Dune House Cozy Mystery Series

Cindy Bell

This is a work of fiction. The characters, incidents and locations portrayed in this book and the names herein are fictitious. Any similarity to or identification with the locations, names, characters or history of any person, product or entity is entirely coincidental and unintentional.

All trademarks and brands referred to in this book are for illustrative purposes only, are the property of their respective owners and not affiliated with this publication in any way. Any trademarks are being used without permission, and the publication of the trademark is not authorized by, associated with or sponsored by the trademark owner.

ISBN-13: 978-1512201444

ISBN-10: 1512201448

More Cozy Mysteries by Cindy Bell

Dune House Cozy Mysteries

Seaside Secrets

Boats and Bad Guys

Treasured History

Hidden Hideaways

Dodgy Dealings

Sage Gardens Cozy Mysteries

Birthdays Can Be Deadly

Money Can Be Deadly

Wendy the Wedding Planner Cozy Mysteries

Matrimony, Money and Murder

Chefs, Ceremonies and Crimes

Knives and Nuptials

Mice, Marriage and Murder

Heavenly Highland Inn Cozy Mysteries

Murdering the Roses

Dead in the Daisies

Killing the Carnations

Drowning the Daffodils

Suffocating the Sunflowers

Books, Bullets and Blooms

A Deadly serious Gardening Contest

A Bridal Bouquet and a Body

Bekki the Beautician Cozy Mysteries

Hairspray and Homicide

A Dyed Blonde and a Dead Body

Mascara and Murder

Pageant and Poison

Conditioner and a Corpse

Mistletoe, Makeup and Murder

Hairpin, Hair Dryer and Homicide

Blush, a Bride and a Body

Shampoo and a Stiff

Cosmetics, a Cruise and a Killer

Lipstick, a Long Iron and Lifeless

Camping, Concealer and Criminals

Table of Contents

Chapter One

Dune House was still. It was very quiet. So quiet that Suzie was sure her footsteps were excessively loud. With the phone in her hand Suzie crept around the corner of the hallway and into the dining room which overlooked the beach. She pressed the phone close to her ear.

"Ma'am, ma'am, are you still there?" a woman's voice was asking.

"Yes, I'm here," Suzie replied in a whisper.

Suzie curved the phone close to her lips. She whispered again into the receiver. "I just want to confirm the flights I reserved," she explained.

"Excuse me, ma'am?" the voice on the other side of the phone asked. "Can you speak up a little?"

"No, I can't," Suzie said with a hiss. She glanced over her shoulder to make sure that Mary hadn't stepped inside. She noticed Mary and

Detective Wes Brown walking along the beach, hand in hand, she breathed in slightly. “Okay,” Suzie said with a sigh of relief. “Sorry about that, it's a surprise,” she explained.

“Okay,” the woman on the other end of the phone said with a hint of annoyance. “So, what can I do for you?”

“I just want to confirm the flights for two passengers,” Suzie explained. She lowered her voice once more and spoke the names of the passengers. She was doing everything she could to keep this surprise a secret.

“Yes, the flights are reserved and paid in full,” the woman replied politely.

“Wonderful, thank you,” Suzie said before hanging up the phone. She was so excited at the thought of seeing Mary's children, and she knew that Mary would be as well. With them both being in college, she wasn't expecting anything special for her birthday. After all Mary had been through with her difficult marriage, Suzie wanted Mary's first birthday as a free woman to be a great celebration. A few minutes later the side door that led to the beach swung open, and Mary stepped inside. Suzie smiled when she saw her.

"How are you this morning?" she asked.

"I'd rather not say," Mary replied sullenly and walked into the kitchen.

"Mary?" Suzie asked as she followed after her. Mary was usually always cheerful. "Are you okay?"

"I'm fine," Mary sighed and started a pot of coffee.

"You don't seem fine," Suzie pointed out. Then she paused a moment. She remembered how depressed she would get around her birthdays. Suzie didn't like growing old, and she could understand that Mary might be a little down about turning another year older. "Is it your birthday?" she asked. "You know that you're only as old as you feel. You're still beautiful, and you will be beautiful for years to come."

"Thank you," Mary said with a small smile. "But that's not it," she shook her head. "I've never dreaded getting older. Now, especially when I have the chance to start my life over."

"Then what is it?" Suzie asked with concern. "I know something is wrong, Mary. You know that you can't hide it from me."

"I know," Mary smiled fondly at Suzie. "I never have been able to."

"So, out with it," Suzie demanded. "What's going on?"

"It's Wes," she explained hesitantly. "I know that things are different now, than they were when I was dating so long ago. But he just seems distant lately. He's always taking these phone calls. Even now when we were walking, he stopped to talk. He always makes sure I can't hear him when he does," she sighed. "I guess I thought my second chance at romance, was going to be real romance. You know the kind that sweeps you off your feet. A man who stares deeply into your eyes, and whispers in your ear, not into his cell phone."

"I'm sorry, Mary," Suzie said softly. "Maybe he's working on a case," she suggested. "You know they have to be pretty private about that."

"I don't think so," Mary frowned. "I asked him if he had been busy at work, and he said that it had been very slow."

"Well, I'm sure there's an explanation," Suzie insisted. "Wes is a good guy, I don't think he would be stringing you along."

"So, what if he's not?" Mary shook her head. "Then he's just bored with me?"

"Who could be bored with someone like you?"

"Maybe I'm just expecting too much," Mary muttered and finished her coffee.

"Maybe we just need to have some time out of this house," Suzie suggested. "We haven't been to the library in some time. I have some books to take back, do you want to keep me company?"

“I'd love that,” Mary agreed with a small sigh. “Maybe I just need a new perspective on things.”

Suzie nodded and patted her hand lightly. As they headed out to the library she kept her eye out for any sign of Detective Brown lurking around the property. She knew that Mary had some of the best instincts she had ever known, and Suzie was highly protective of her. As they drove towards the library, Mary had a vague look of sadness.

“Mary, cheer up, it's your birthday soon,” Suzie said. She turned the car onto the main street of town.

“I know,” Mary sighed. “I'm sure we'll have fun. I guess it's these times of the year that make me feel a little left behind.”

“You're not left behind,” Suzie argued. “You're running your own business...”

“Your business,” Mary pointed out.

“Our business,” Suzie said firmly. “You know the bed and breakfast wouldn't exist without you, Mary. Don't you?” she glanced over to meet her friend's eyes.

"I guess," Mary replied. "Don't get me wrong, I love Dune House, it's just a transitional time for me."

"I understand," Suzie said. She wished she did. Mary's life had always been so different from her own, and yet they had always been able to connect, even when Suzie was off in some foreign country chasing down a story and Mary was debating cloth or disposable diapers. They were more than friends, they were sisters, even if they didn't share blood. "But this could be a good transition," Suzie pointed out. "You get to choose what comes next."

"I thought I would love that," Mary laughed. "It's a lot harder than I expected it to be."

"You'll figure it out," Suzie said with confidence. "I know it's just words, but I know that you will find your way."

"I appreciate that," Mary said and nudged her arm lightly. "If I get lost, at least I'll have you to snap me out of it."

"Oh, I will," Suzie chuckled. "Trust me, I will."

***

The parking lot of the library was mostly empty. It wasn't the most popular place in the seaside tourist town. The local museum and wide variety of restaurants were much more popular. For that reason it was fairly small. But because of the head librarian, it had one of the best collections of books. Suzie had yet to find anything she couldn't get at the library. She held the door open for Mary as they walked inside. Suzie knew that something was up when she walked into the library. Louis usually had his nose buried in a book, but today he was pacing back and forth. He had a glow in his cheeks. His eyes were shining behind his glasses.

"Hi Louis," Suzie said as she walked up to the desk. Mary offered him a friendly smile.

"Hello ladies," Louis said with a wide grin. "I'm so glad that you're here. I have some amazing news."

"What is it?" Suzie asked, her own excitement building.

"A few months ago a mentor of mine passed away. He and I were good friends in college," he explained.

"How is that good news?" Mary asked with surprise.

"That's not the good news," Louis said sharply. "They finally got his estate straightened out. I had no idea he intended to leave me anything. But he did. I might as well have won the lottery!"

"That much money?" Suzie asked, her eyes wide. "What a windfall!"

"Oh, it is quite a windfall, but it isn't money," Louis smiled. "It's a book."

"A book?" Mary shook her head. "You're this happy about a book?"

"It's not just any book," he sighed. "It's a rare

antique book, one of a kind. Collectors all over the world fight over the chance to get their hands on this book, and Richard left it to me," he said proudly.

"Congratulations, Louis," Mary said warmly. "That really is a treasure."

"It isn't just the book," Louis admitted. "It's that Richard chose me to give it to. I didn't see him for a few months before he died. I tried to visit him, but his family kept him very secluded. It means the world to me that he thought enough of me that he wanted me to have the book."

"I'm very happy for you, Louis," Suzie said. "I'd love to have the chance to see it sometime."

"That would be lovely," Mary agreed.

Louis stared at them both for a long moment. Then he nodded shortly. He gestured for them both to follow him. Mary and Suzie exchanged confused looks, but they followed after Louis. Louis paused beside the employees' only door, and looked back at them both.

“Now, this is completely against the rules. I'm trusting you both not to get me into any trouble,” he raised an eyebrow as he looked at them.

“No trouble,” Suzie promised.

“Quiet as mice,” Mary added with a genuine smile.

“Okay,” he sighed and opened the door. Suzie swept her gaze over the large office that they walked into. It was set up more as a living room than an office, with overstuffed furniture as well as many coffee tables. There were piles of books all over the room. On one table, there was a large wooden box.

“Nice place,” Suzie said with a smile. “I had no idea all of this was in here.”

“It's a retreat,” Louis explained. “Just a place where the staff can go to enjoy a book.”

“What's this?” Mary asked as she peered at the box.

“Careful,” Louis warned. “That's where the book is.”

Mary and Suzie raised eyebrows at each other. Suzie thought it was quite a lot of trouble to go to for a book.

Louis carefully lifted the lid of the box. Then he picked up some rubber gloves and slid them on his hands. He reached inside the box and cautiously lifted the book out of the box. Suzie didn't know what to expect, but with all of the fanfare she was thinking it might be jewel encrusted or carved from marble. Instead it was a simple leather bound book that could have been on any shelf. It appeared to be old, but it didn't appear to be special.

“Isn't it beautiful?” Louis asked as he peered at it through his thick glasses.

“It is,” Mary replied wistfully.

Suzie smiled and nodded. She didn't see what the big deal was, but if Louis loved it so much, it mattered to her that it was important to him.

“It's a collection of poems,” he explained. “To be honest I'm not that fond of poetry, but this book has been passed down through generations of families and is one of the oldest books to be in such excellent condition."

"Amazing," Mary sighed.

"It looks like leather," Suzie said and reached out to touch the cover. Louis smacked her hand away before she could touch it.

"Ouch!" Suzie murmured.

"I'm so sorry," Louis said quickly and set the book back down in the box. "It's just that the oils from your skin might cause damage to the book."

"Well, then I'm sorry, too," Suzie said. She was still a little annoyed, but she realized her mistake.

"It's not insured yet," he explained. "That's another reason why I have to be so careful with it. I tried to get it insured based on the information that came with it, but the agency insisted that one of their valuers had to inspect it."

"Make sure you keep it safe until then," Mary said with a smile.

"I plan to, I am taking it home with me today and I actually have a valuer coming out to see the book. It is such a long drive for him to come all the way out here," Louis explained. "I agreed to arrange accommodation for him so I was hoping maybe he could stay at Dune House for the night," he glanced between the two of them.

"Of course," Suzie nodded. "It's no problem at all."

"Great!" Louis said with excitement. "I bet he will love Dune House. With his eye for detail and history I'm sure he will."

"We'll get a room ready for him," Mary offered. "Congratulations, Louis, on receiving such a treasure."

"I can barely believe it myself," Louis shook his head. "When I said goodbye to Richard, I never thought I'd be receiving this book from him. It was hard to lose him, but he'd been sick for so long," he frowned as he swept his gaze over the book. "I guess even more than the historical value of this book, is the sentimental value. A valuer can't put a price on that, can he?"

"No, I don't think so," Suzie said warmly. "It's nice to have something that will remind you of your friend."

"Yes, it is," Louis said with a smile. "Thanks again. The valuer's name is Warren Blasser. He should be arriving around six tonight."

"Great," Suzie nodded. "We'll be ready for him."

As Suzie and Mary walked out of the library, Suzie caught sight of Jason's patrol car rolling down the main street. She lifted her hand and waved to him. He flashed his lights back at her.

"He just loves playing with those lights," Suzie laughed and shook her head.

"I would, too," Mary grinned. "And the siren."

"Wouldn't it be so much fun to take it for a spin around town?" Suzie suggested. "I'm sure Jason wouldn't mind."

"I'm sure he would," Mary burst out laughing. "But he'd have a hard time catching us without his car."

"Let's do it," Suzie said mischievously. "What's the worst that could happen?"

"We could be arrested by your young cousin and miss the chance to host Warren Blasser," Mary pointed out.

"Oh Mary," Suzie sighed with disappointment. "You're always so reasonable."

"Someone has to be," Mary said teasingly. "You've been getting me into trouble since high school."

Suzie offered an innocent smile as they settled into her car.

"Sometimes it's fun to do something completely unexpected," Suzie pointed out as she started the car.

"Yes, like ice cream for breakfast, or swimming at midnight, but not stealing a cop car, Suzie, really?" she raised an eyebrow. "What's brought on this daring behavior?"

"I don't know," Suzie said grimly. "I guess that I've been feeling a little restless. With the renovations complete on Dune House and tourist season behind us, sometimes I feel like I'm dusting the same furniture over and over again."

"That's because you are," Mary grinned. "But the rest of the furniture could use a dusting, too, you know."

"Ha," Suzie smiled at her friend. "I mean, it's great when Paul is here, but he ships out tomorrow for a few days. I feel like while he's gone I have nothing to do with myself."

"Well, since Wes seems to be otherwise occupied, we can always do something fun together," Mary suggested. As she spoke her cell phone began to ring. She smirked as she looked at the name on the phone. "I guess he really is a good detective," she said. "Hello?"

"Mary, sorry I had to take off this morning," Wes said quickly. "I want to make up for it. Can we have dinner tonight?”

Mary gulped. She covered the receiver of the phone.

“He wants to have dinner,” she whispered to Suzie.

“Make him work for it,” Suzie advised.

Mary nodded. “Well, I'm a little busy tonight,” Mary said mildly. “It is very short notice after all.”

“I know,” he sighed into the phone. “If you're too busy we can do it another time. I was just hoping to get some time with you.”

“I think maybe I could swing it,” Mary said quietly. Suzie winked at her.

“Oh great, how about six?” he suggested.

“Wait just a minute,” Mary said. She covered the phone again. “He wants to have dinner at six, but Warren should be arriving about then.”

“I'll be fine,” Suzie assured her. “It'll be fun to have something to do!”

“All right,” Mary laughed a little. She

uncovered the phone. "You can pick me up at six."

"Thanks Mary, I'm looking forward to it," Wes said before hanging up the phone.

"See," Suzie said with a smile. "He's making dates with you, he's obviously interested."

"Or he wants to let me down easy in a public place," Mary pointed out.

"If he does, he's an idiot," Suzie said as she pulled the car into the long driveway at Dune House. The beautiful old structure rose up regally against the sky. Where it stood perched above the beach it looked like it had a bird's eye view of the entire town. Suzie stared at it for a moment, still amazed that it belonged to her. She and Mary had turned it back into its former glory as a bed and breakfast, and the business was steady. But that wasn't why Suzie loved it. She loved it because it was something that she and Mary had created together. She glanced over at Mary and smiled as the woman fumbled with her purse and the door handle of the car.

Mary was one of the kindest, gentlest people she knew. Luckily, she was best friends with Suzie, who would defend her against anyone who tried to hurt her. Mary had a far more gentle approach to things than Suzie, so sometimes Suzie felt as if she needed to step in and be a little more forceful in order to shield her. Of course that had led to a few disagreements between them. But as she watched Mary walk up towards the front entrance of Dune House, Suzie felt that familiar surge, the need to protect her. Suzie only hoped that she was being paranoid.

Chapter Two

After returning to Dune House, Suzie spent a little time tidying up her room. She and Mary both lived in the B & B. Suzie had decorated each room in a different style. They each had their own theme. She was constantly redecorating her own room. Her most recent theme was nautical with shells, old maps, and vintage pictures of beach paradises. It made her feel a little closer to her boyfriend, Paul, who was often out on the water as he was a professional fisherman. However, the sand mural she had been attempting to create had turned into a complete disaster, which included sand being stuck in between the wooden slats of the flooring in her room.

Suzie was working on getting the sand free when she heard the sound of the doorbell ringing. She had locked up because they did not have any guests, and they were not expecting Warren Blasser until later in the evening. When she reached the door the person outside had already rung the doorbell quite a few more times. She peeked through the windows that framed the door and saw a man standing outside. He was short in stature, a little on the heavy side, and wearing a nice suit. Suzie didn't recognize him and so she guessed that he was not a local. She unlocked the door and opened it.

"How can I help you?" she asked in a friendly tone.

"Do you have a room available?" the man asked breathlessly as he stepped inside. Suzie regarded him skeptically. They didn't often get guests on the spur of the moment as they usually called ahead to reserve a room. However, there were several rooms available, so she decided it couldn't hurt.

"Sure," she said. "Let me just get some information from you and we'll get you all set up."

"Great," he said as he followed her to the front desk. "I'm sorry to just show up, but my other reservation fell through."

"Are you visiting Garber?" Suzie asked as she opened up the registration form on the computer.

"Passing through," he replied. She looked up at him again. She was fairly cautious about her guests. This man seemed a little sketchy, but he spoke politely and his eyes seemed kind enough.

"Your name please?" she asked.

"John," he said quickly. "John Richardson," he added. Suzie typed the name into the computer.

"How long do you think you will be staying?" she asked.

"Probably just the night," he said. "Maybe two," he shrugged a little. "I'm paying cash so I'll pay for the first night now."

"Okay," Suzie smiled warmly as he handed her the money. "My name is Suzie, if you need anything. We offer breakfast, lunch, and dinner. Of course there are many wonderful local restaurants."

“Thanks,” he nodded. “My room?”

“You'll be in room seven,” she said and handed him a key. “I'll show you the way.”

“Thank you,” he said.

“Did you want to get your luggage?” she asked.

“I don't have any,” he replied vaguely.

Suzie considered asking him why he didn't have any luggage, but she didn't want to be too nosy. She led him to the room which was on the second floor. She opened the door for him.

“The phone will dial to the desk if you need anything,” she explained.

“Great,” he nodded. “I really just need some rest.”

“Well, you'll get plenty of that here,” Suzie said with a warm smile.

“Wonderful,” he said. He stepped into the room and closed the door behind him. Suzie lingered for a moment outside the door, then headed back down to the first floor to finish checking him in. When she reached the first floor, she ran into Mary who was nervously straightening her skirt.

"You look beautiful," Suzie said as she walked up to her.

"I feel frumpy," Mary admitted with a sigh. She brushed her auburn hair back from her eyes and frowned. "Who ever thought dating at my age was a good idea?" she asked.

"At your age?" Suzie clucked her tongue. "Mary, don't let your birthday get to you. You are a beautiful, amazing woman and Wes is lucky that you even look in his direction."

"That's sweet of you to say, Suzie, but I don't know that he feels the same way," she bit into her bottom lip. "Things are so different now. When we were young if someone dated you, they dated you, only you, and there weren't all these questions to think about. I have no idea whether we are even really dating. Are we exclusive? Are we friends?

What does he expect?"

"Wow, wait a minute," Suzie said and rested her hands lightly on Mary's shoulders. "You need to take a breath. Dating is supposed to be fun, remember?" she asked as she looked into her eyes.

"To be honest, Suzie, I'm about ready to call it all off," Mary frowned. "Maybe I'm just being paranoid, but it seems like Wes is losing interest."

"Maybe you need to give it a little time, Mary," Suzie suggested. "You and Wes haven't been dating that long. He doesn't seem that confident with romance either," she pointed out. She took a breath and then looked into Mary's eyes. "Not every man is going to be Kent, Mary, I promise."

"You can promise, but that doesn't mean it's true," Mary shook her head. "Maybe it was foolish of me to think I was ready to start another relationship."

"Not foolish at all," Suzie insisted. "Just try to relax a little and see what happens. Talk to Wes about it, ask him to define what is happening between the two of you. He's probably just as nervous as you are."

"Maybe," Mary took a deep breath. "I think you're right. I'll talk to him about it tonight. It can't hurt to ask, right?" she smiled a little.

"Good," Suzie nodded. "If he gives you a hard time, just send me a text, and I'll hunt him down," she offered.

Mary grinned at her. "I think you actually would."

"Oh, you know I would," Suzie said and hugged Mary gently. "You look gorgeous," she said again. There was a light knock at the front door. The door pushed open, and Wes stepped inside. He was wearing a nice gray suit, and for once he had shoes on instead of cowboy boots. His silver-black hair was combed neatly. His expression was as difficult to read as ever.

"Evening ladies," he said as he stepped inside.

"Hi Wes," Mary smiled a little. Suzie raised an

eyebrow and stared at him. He stared back at her for a moment. He looked a little confused and then smiled at Mary.

"You look stunning," he said warmly.

"Thank you," Mary replied. He stepped up to her and offered her his arm.

"Ready to go?" he asked. He cast a wary glance in Suzie's direction.

"Yes," Mary said and wrapped her arm around his. "Thanks, Suzie," Mary said.

"Just remember what I said," Suzie said. "Text me."

"I will," Mary laughed.

"It was nice to see you, Suzie," Wes said and offered her a polite nod.

"You, too," Suzie replied but she didn't smile. Wes stared at her again as if he was trying to figure out why she was being abrupt. Then he shook his head and began leading Mary out of Dune House. Suzie overheard him murmuring to her.

“What was all that about?” he asked.

“Oh you know Suzie,” Mary said warmly. “She's always looking out for me.”

Suzie smiled at her friend's words. After the door closed behind the two she set about preparing for their next guest's arrival.

Chapter Three

Not long after Mary left, there was another knock at the door. Suzie had just finished pouring herself a cup of tea. She left it on the counter as she walked towards the door to answer it. Unlike the earlier guest, the person waiting outside did not repeatedly ring the doorbell. Suzie opened the door and smiled at the man who stood outside. He was tall and very thin. The type of body that she would describe as willowy. His hair was thin and wispy, light brown in color. He had a long nose, and thin lips arranged in a serious expression.

“May I help you?” Suzie asked.

“Yes, my name's Warren Blasser,” he replied in an even tone. He spoke as if each word was carefully selected. “I was told there would be a room here for me.”

“There is,” Suzie smiled warmly. “Welcome, please come in,” she stepped aside so that he could walk in. He had a small overnight bag as well as a soft-sided briefcase. “How was your drive?” she asked as she walked over to the reception desk.

“It was fine,” he said with a slight shrug.

“Would you like anything to eat or drink?” she offered as she opened up the registration form on the computer.

“I had something along the way,” he explained. “Really, I'd just like to rest up a bit.”

“Okay, well I'll get you right to your room then,” Suzie offered as she tapped in some of his information on the computer. “My name is Suzie, if you need anything,” she added. “We provide breakfast, lunch, and dinner,” she continued.

“I'm not much for breakfast,” the man explained as Suzie began to lead him towards the stairs. She noticed the way his eyes were roaming over the interior of the house. “Just some coffee will be fine.”

“Certainly,” she nodded. “I'll make sure that there is a fresh pot.”

She paused at the bottom of the stairs. Warren had stopped in the middle of the living room area. His gaze was settled on the light fixtures.

“Remarkable,” he said in a whisper. “Are these original to the house?” he asked.

“I believe so,” Suzie nodded. “We had to do some rewiring of course.”

“Of course,” he nodded and continued to study them. “I am always so pleased to see people take the time to preserve the past,” he said. “There's so much that is just swept away, without people ever noticing the value in what they are bulldozing.”

“That's true,” Suzie smiled a little. “We tried not to do that too much here.”

“I can see that,” he said with appreciation. “So much is lost already to natural disasters and the destruction of wars, it makes such a difference to put in a little extra effort to let things remain as they are. I've seen many old homes turned into bed and breakfasts or restaurants, and the owners practically gut them," he cringed at the idea.

"Hopefully that will never happen here," Suzie said. "I personally think that the structure and design of an old home holds many secrets, things that the people of the time when it was built didn't write down, but are still conveyed through the things they built and how they built them."

"Exactly," he said with a breath of relief. His hand lingered on the railing as they began to go up the stairs. She noticed his look of disappointment.

"Unfortunately, some things had to be replaced for the sake of safety," Suzie explained. "I wish the original structure could have lasted forever, but I wouldn't want any of my guests to be hurt either."

"Some things can't be avoided," he agreed. "At least you haven't plastered the fireplaces with plasma televisions or cut out skylights to appease the tourists."

Suzie laughed at the idea. “That would be a little absurd wouldn't it?”

“You'd be surprised,” he said as they paused outside the room that he was staying in. “I once stayed in a bed and breakfast that boasted it was built in the civil war era. They had a spa bath, a television that hung from the ceiling and was nearly as wide as the bed, and heated floors. I'm not sure what any of that had to do with the civil war.”

“Me neither,” Suzie laughed again. She was enjoying her talk with Warren. It wasn't often that she had the chance to pick the mind of a history buff. She opened the door to the room for him. She had chosen it specifically for him. It was the room she had designed to be an 'antique' room. Everything used to decorate the room was purchased locally from antique shops, estate sales, and roadside stands.

“How beautiful,” he said with a secretive smile as if he knew that she had chosen it just for him. Suzie walked over to the curtains and drew them apart, revealing an uninterrupted view of the sea.

"Amazing," he breathed as he walked towards the window. Suzie thought he was talking about the view, but his eyes were locked on the intricate wall hanging beside the window. Suzie smiled to herself. Warren Blasser was certainly proof that beauty was in the eye of the beholder.

"There's a balcony," she explained. "Just make sure you lock the door when you turn in for the night."

"I will," he said. He seemed to be enthralled by a small statue he had picked up off one of the shelves. Suzie was glad that he was enjoying the room.

"I hope you enjoy your stay," Suzie said. "The telephone will dial the desk if you need anything."

"Uh huh, thank you," he nodded, obviously distracted. She stepped out of the room and headed back down the stairs to the first floor. She had some birthday planning to catch up on. Now that she had confirmed the flights for Benjamin and Catherine, Mary's son and daughter, she had to make sure the caterer was going to show and that the bakery was working on the cake. Suzie wanted everything to be just perfect for Mary. She only hoped that the gesture would show her just how special she was to Suzie. She had just finished the last of her phone calls when she heard a sound outside the door. She wondered if it might be another unexpected guest. When she checked the clock she saw that it was a little after seven. She walked over to the door just as it was swinging open. She felt a little fearful as she wasn't expecting anyone to just walk in. But when she saw Mary step through the door, her fear melted into sympathy.

"Mary, what are you doing home so early?" Suzie asked as she walked up to her friend. Mary closed the door firmly.

"He got a phone call," she said in a tight voice. "He said it was an emergency and sent me home in a taxi before we had even gotten our order."

"Oh Mary, I'm sorry," Suzie said and hugged her. "Maybe it was an emergency, maybe it was work," she suggested.

"No, it wasn't," Mary said with certainty. "He was smiling, Suzie. I can't believe I let myself be so foolish as to believe that he would really want to be with me. I can tell you this much, I'm not going to be somebody's pet that they pick up when they feel like it. As far as I'm concerned Wes can go find someone else to send home in a taxi," she spat out each word. Suzie had never seen Mary so angry, unless it was after a fight with Kent. Her heart broke for her friend that she was experiencing this kind of frustration again.

"Maybe..." Suzie started to say.

"No," Mary said sternly. "Sorry, Suzie, but I don't want to talk about it anymore. I just want to go to bed," she sighed and marched off to her room.

Suzie watched her go. Her blood began to boil as she thought of Wes. She had been wary of him from the start, but then he had seemed to reveal himself as a decent and thoughtful man. Now she felt differently. She wondered if all of the kindness was a smokescreen he had thrown up just to draw Mary in. Suzie was beside herself with anger. She wanted to protect her friend.

Suzie hesitantly walked up to Mary's room. She listened for a moment. She could hear Mary crying quietly. It was a terrible sound for Suzie to hear. It made her furious. She wanted to open the door and hold her friend tightly in her arms, but she knew better. Mary often liked to be left alone when she was upset. If she wanted company she would ask. Suzie frowned and walked away from her room. She went so far as to pick up her phone and dial Wes' number. It went to voicemail right away as if he had turned off his phone. "Aargh," Suzie growled in frustration and hung up the phone.

"Everything okay?" a voice asked from behind her. She spun around quickly to discover Warren standing behind her. She blushed, embarrassed that he had seen her so angry.

"I'm so sorry," she said. "I didn't know you were there."

"No need to apologize," he said with a small smile. "We all have those moments. Is there anything I can do to help?"

Suzie smiled at him. She thought his offer was very sweet. "Thank you, but it involves matters of the heart, you know how that goes," she laughed a little.

"Not really," he admitted. "I've never been terribly interested in them."

Suzie raised an eyebrow. "Well, lucky for you," she said with genuine admiration. "They are very murky waters."

"Indeed," he nodded. "I was just going to take a walk along the beach. Would you like to join me?"

Suzie stared at him for a moment. The invitation was unexpected. She couldn't tell if he was just being friendly, or if he wanted something more from her. She wondered if she had done anything to give him the impression that she would be interested. She didn't think Paul would appreciate her taking an evening walk on the beach with a man she barely knew. Of course, she was a free woman.

“I'm sorry I have some other things I have to do right now,” Suzie said quickly.

“No problem,” he nodded. “I just thought it might help you calm down if you got some fresh air.”

“Thank you,” she said. “I think I'll just find my tea and try to relax. You should walk to the north, there are some flat rocks that you could sit on and see the stars.”

“Thanks for the tip,” he said. He offered her a quick nod and then headed off down the hallway. Suzie was about to try calling Wes again when her phone began ringing in her hand. She saw that it was Paul. Despite the fact that she had declined the invite to go on the walk she still felt a little guilty as she answered the phone.

"Hey sweetie," she said softly.

"Hello beautiful," he replied. She grinned. She had always teased her friends about the cutesy names they would use with their boyfriends or husbands, but now she understood how it could make you smile no matter how silly it was.

"How are you doing?" she asked as she leaned back against the wall and sighed.

"I'd be better if I was with you," he replied in a sultry tone.

"Well, that can be arranged, can't it?" Suzie said with a soft laugh.

"Do you have guests?" he asked.

"I do, but they are settled. I can spend a few minutes on the porch with you," she assured him.

"Perfect," he said swiftly. "I can be there in about ten minutes."

"I'll be waiting for you," Suzie replied happily. As she hung up the phone she felt a familiar excitement that was only triggered when Paul was on his way to see her. She headed out to the front porch to wait for him. She looked up at the sky which was filled with stars. As she leaned against the railing of the front porch she gazed up at the rising moon. Sometimes in the bustle of life she forgot just how breathtaking the view from Dune House could be. She had been to many beautiful places, but there was something special about Garber, and the small stretch of beach that it claimed. Maybe it was the lack of tourist traps, or maybe it was the surprising quiet in the evenings, all she knew for sure was that she had never felt more at peace.

When Suzie heard the rumble of an engine she turned back to the parking lot, expecting it to be Paul pulling in. However, the car that slowly rolled past was not one that she recognized. It was a dusty mustard color. It moved so slowly that it left her unsettled. Then she watched as it nestled itself in the thick brush on the side of the parking lot. Suzie was sure that the driver hadn't seen her.

She hadn't turned on the porch light as she didn't want to disturb either of her guests. But obviously the driver was up to something suspicious. She was halfway down the driveway when she saw another pair of headlights pulling in. This time it was Paul. He pulled up beside her and rolled down the window.

"What are you doing out here?" he asked as she continued to walk past him.

"Did you see that car when you pulled in?" she asked, distracted.

"What car?" he frowned and parked the car. Suzie was still walking to the end of the driveway when Paul caught up with her. "Where are you going?" he asked. He was obviously confused.

"There was a car that just pulled in. It's hidden in the brush," she said and pointed to the subtle glow of the taillights.

"What's it doing back there?" Paul said as he craned his neck. "Did it look familiar?"

"No, I've never seen it before, not even around

town," Suzie said.

"Well, let's see if we can find out what's going on," Paul said and wrapped his arm around her. Just as they were about to get to the car, it suddenly pulled out. It spun around and then slammed on the gas. It tore down the road before Suzie could get a glimpse of the license plate.

"Wow, he's going somewhere in a rush," Paul said with a growl in his voice.

"I wonder where to?" Suzie shook her head.

"Doesn't matter now," Paul said. "He's already gone."

"Don't you think it was odd though?" she asked as she met his eyes.

"Very," Paul agreed. "But maybe he was just lost and looking at his map or something," he suggested. As they walked back towards the porch, Paul pulled her a little closer. "Try not to worry about it."

"How could I worry with you here?" she asked with a slow smile.

"That's a nice thing to say," he said and helped her up onto the porch.

"It's the truth," she replied and smiled warmly at him. "I'm glad you're here."

"Well, that makes two of us," he said and hugged her.

"I wish you didn't have to go back out so soon," she admitted.

"I know, but I'll be back in time for the party," he pointed out and met her eyes. "I think that it is going to be great."

"I hope so," Suzie nodded. She was still a little distracted by the car she had seen.

"Don't worry so much, Suzie," he kissed her cheek gently. "Everything is going to be just fine."

"Maybe it will," Suzie said grimly.

"Just relax, it will all be okay," he gave her a soft kiss before pulling slightly away.

"Thank you, I hope you're right," Suzie said and kissed him again.

"I better get going," Paul sighed. "I have to prepare the boat for shipping out."

"Thank you for the visit," Suzie smiled.

"Can we have dinner tomorrow night?" Paul asked. "I know you have guests, but I'd love to see you before I launch."

"I'm sure Mary will be willing to handle things," Suzie nodded.

"Great," Paul smiled. "If you see that car again make sure you call Jason to check it out," he said sternly. Then he turned and walked away. Suzie watched him go until the headlights of his car pulled out of the parking lot.

"Now, I see why you turned down the walk," a voice said from behind her.

"Warren," Suzie said as she turned to face him with a smile.

"Looks like you've got a good man there," he said with a half-smile.

"The best," Suzie nodded.

“Well, I'm going to turn in for the night. Nice beach you have here,” he said before he turned and walked back into Dune House. Suzie lingered for a few minutes on the porch. She was waiting to see if the car would drive by again. The street in front of Dune House remained quiet.

Chapter Four

Eventually Suzie went back inside. She wanted to check on Mary. When she paused outside her door she still heard quiet crying. Suzie raised her hand to knock, but then stopped herself. It was hard for Suzie to resist, but she forced herself to walk towards her room. She felt a surge of fury rush through her as she blamed Wes for causing her friend such pain. She was very tempted to get in her car, drive over to his place, and teach him what happens when someone messes with Mary. But Suzie knew that Mary wouldn't want that either. She sighed as she stretched out in her bed. She closed her eyes and tried to distract herself with thoughts of the party, but her mind kept returning to Wes and how hurt Mary was.

She was so concerned and angry that she couldn't get to sleep. She lay awake for hours after she went to bed. As she was tossing and turning, she heard a scream. Suzie bolted up out of bed at the sound. It was followed by a loud thump. Her heart jumped up into her throat. She didn't know what had happened, but she was sure it was bad. She grabbed her phone and opened her door. When Suzie ran out into the hall Mary was already there. Her eyes were wide.

"Did you hear that?" she asked in a hushed voice.

"I did," Suzie replied.

"I'll check upstairs," Mary said.

"I'll check outside," Suzie called back as she ran for the door. The thump had sounded like it came from the side of Dune House. As she ran across the sand, her feet slipped a few times. She was more tired than she had realized. But that sensation of exhaustion disappeared entirely when she came upon a body laying face down in the sand.

"Oh no!" she shouted as she realized it was Warren.

"Suzie, is he alive?" Mary called down from the balcony of Warren's room. Suzie looked up to see that the railing was swinging free. Nervously she reached down to touch the side of Warren's neck. Her eyes misted with tears as she felt no sign of a pulse. Suzie's stomach clenched with dread as she gave in to what she already knew to be true.

"I don't think so," Suzie said. "I think he's gone."

"This is unreal!" Mary called out. "I'll be right down!"

"I better call Jason," Suzie said more to herself than to Mary.

"Jason, I'm sorry, I know it's late," Suzie said quickly into the phone. "We have a big problem here, I need the police out here right away. One of our guests is dead."

"What?" Jason spat back, his voice becoming more alert. "I'll send everybody out, I'll be there in just a few minutes. Are you safe?"

"Yes, I don't know what happened," Suzie said

tearfully. “I don't know what happened,” she repeated, panic starting to rise in her voice.

“Just try to stay calm, I'll be there in a few minutes,” he promised before hanging up the phone. Suzie hung up as well. Mary emerged from the side door of Dune House and rushed over to Suzie. Waves crashed hard against the beach, moistening the air with their spray. Suzie felt a sense of emptiness in the darkness that surrounded her.

“How could this happen?” Mary asked with disbelief as she stared down at the body. “Is that the insurance man?”

“Warren Blasser,” Suzie said softly, her voice trembling. “He was such an interesting person. So nice.”

“What are we going to do, Suzie?” Mary asked as she looked up at the broken railing. “How could the railing have given way? Is this our fault?” she asked with a gasp.

“Someone must have shoved him into it,”

Suzie said with a slow shake of her head. "It couldn't have given way on its own. I know it couldn't. We had all of the railings and balconies inspected."

Sirens screamed through the early morning darkness shattering the silence that filled the space between them. Suzie shivered and wrapped her arms around herself. She wondered how this was going to be handled.

"Mary, stay close to me," Suzie said with some urgency in her voice. "The killer may still be in Dune House, or at the very least nearby."

"I'm not going anywhere," Mary assured her. She looked warily around at the sprawling stretch of sand. It was empty for the moment, but that didn't mean that somebody hadn't been there only moments before.

Three police cars and an ambulance skidded into the parking lot. One officer, Suzie's cousin, Jason, climbed out and ran across the sand to reach Suzie's side.

"Are you okay?" he asked breathlessly. The paramedics rushed past him to confirm that Warren was indeed dead.

"I think so, Jason," Suzie said. "I have no idea what happened. I couldn't sleep, I heard a scream, and then..."

Jason peered up at the railing. "I thought you had those updated?" he asked with an edge to his voice. "I told you to make sure that you did."

"I did," Suzie insisted. "We tried to keep the look as authentic as possible, but every balcony was updated and inspected. Someone must have pushed him off. The murderer must still be on the loose and may be nearby. You have to send officers to search the beach."

Jason frowned and lifted his hat off his red hair. "It doesn't look like a murder, Suzie. It looks like he leaned on the railing and it broke, allowing him to fall."

"That's not true," Suzie insisted. "Like I said all of the balconies are solid."

Jason waved to one of the other officers who was jogging towards the entrance of Dune House. Then he glanced over at Suzie with some concern. "Maybe you missed one," he said.

"Excuse me?" Suzie asked defensively. "I didn't miss any balconies. When I inherited this house I knew your father had let it get run-down, I had this place inspected from top to bottom and you know that, Jason," Suzie was really starting to get aggravated.

Jason frowned. "I know," he said quietly. "I know this is all very upsetting. I'm not trying to make it harder on you. But mistakes can happen, Suzie."

"It wasn't a mistake," Suzie insisted with frustration. "The car!" she suddenly announced.

"What car?" Jason asked, obviously confused.

"I saw a car driving by the parking lot really slow earlier this evening. It parked in the brush by the driveway. It must have been the killer."

"The killer?" Jason frowned again. "Suzie, just

take a breath, I think you're getting ahead of yourself."

"Jason, you can believe what you want, but this was a murder," Suzie huffed.

"I'm going to take a closer look, then maybe we can figure out what happened," Jason said and walked away from her towards Dune House. Suzie watched him step into the home that used to belong to his father. She respected Jason as a police officer, and as her cousin, but she didn't like what he was implying. If he was so quick to assume that it was an accident, which might imply that it was due to negligence on her part, then wouldn't everyone else be quick to assume the same thing?

"What did he say?" Mary asked as she walked away from the paramedics and over to Suzie.

"He thinks the railing gave way," Suzie said darkly. "He thinks it was nothing more than an accident."

"Well, that is how it looks," Mary said as she

watched the officers step carefully out onto the balcony.

"You know that's not possible, Mary," Suzie said and turned to look at her friend. "Don't you?"

"I do," Mary agreed. "I was here for the inspection, I saw it with my own eyes."

"I'm sure they're going to find some evidence of someone else throwing Warren off the balcony. But the question is why?"

"A murder at Dune House," Mary sighed. "Even after we prove that it wasn't our fault, we are going to take a hit for this. Good thing it is after tourist season."

"That's one good thing at least," Suzie replied as she watched the officers inspecting the loose railing. "But, I have a feeling we're going to need all the help that we can get with this."

"I think so, too," Mary agreed. "I'll be back in a second, I'm just going to see that John hasn't been woken by the commotion." She walked back into the house. Suzie realized that she was still in her loose nightgown with all of these people around her. She shivered in the cool breeze that was coming off the water.

“Here,” Jason said from beside her. She hadn't even seen him come back outside. He draped his jacket around her.

“Thank you,” Suzie said quietly. His expression was tight, his eyes narrowed. “What is it Jason?” she asked.

“Suzie, I'm going to have to ask you a few questions,” he said with a frown. “I know that it's going to be awkward, but I have paperwork that I have to fill out before I can wrap this up.”

“Wrap this up?” Suzie asked with shock. “What are you talking about? Do you know who did it?”

“Who did what?” Jason asked. “It was an accident, Suzie.”

“That's impossible,” Suzie frowned.

“Suzie, there is no evidence of the railing being damaged. There's no sign of any struggle in the room, or on the balcony. My best guess is that the victim walked out on the balcony to wait for the sunrise, and when he leaned against the railing, it gave way."

"How could it?" Suzie demanded. "It was sturdy, we had it inspected..."

"It looks like it might have lost a screw or two. Maybe in the high winds we had a couple of weeks ago," he shrugged. "Sometimes the weather does more damage than we realize."

"Jason, there's no way," Suzie insisted. "I check the balconies after every weather event."

"Maybe you overlooked one," Jason said grimly.

"No, I didn't," Suzie said, anger rising in her voice.

"Look Suzie, I know that this is going to put Dune House into a bit of a mess, so I understand why you're upset. But I need to ask you a few questions for the record, so are you going to answer them or should I get one of the other officers?" he narrowed his eyes.

"Fine, fine," Suzie waved her hand. "Ask your questions."

"Did you have any recent complaints from guests about the state of the balconies?" he asked.

"No, of course not," Suzie snapped in return.

"Did you actually see the victim on the balcony before he fell?"

"No," she growled. "I heard a scream, and then a thump, I came running out here to check what it was and found Warren on the ground."

"Okay, I think that should cover it," Jason said as he put away his paperwork. "If you think of anything else to add, just let me know. The victim will be taken to the medical examiner for an autopsy, but pending the results this is being considered an accidental death."

"This is terrible," Suzie muttered under her breath. "Jason, you must know that we would never put anyone in danger."

"All I know is that there is no evidence of a struggle, no evidence of external damage to the balcony, and the only injuries I've seen on the victim are those caused by the fall. You say you had the balconies inspected, I believe you, Suzie. But this is a big house, and one balcony could have been missed, or maybe the damage wasn't noticed. It wasn't a murder," he said flatly. "That means it's not my department anymore."

"It was," Suzie crossed her arms. "Someone killed that poor man and you're going to just write it off as an accident. Jason, you have to do your job and look into it properly," Suzie demanded. As soon as she spoke the words she regretted it. Jason's expression hardened.

"Suzie, just because you don't want it to be accident due to the railing, doesn't mean it isn't," he shot back. He took a deep breath and swept his gaze over the scene which was flooded by flashing lights. "Listen, if anything comes up in the autopsy or any other evidence comes to light, then we can start an appropriate investigation. Until then, the death is considered accidental," he turned and walked away from her. Suzie watched her young cousin go. She was sure she had gone too far with the remark about him doing his job properly. The truth was, he was a good police officer. Suzie knew that. She also knew he could only work from the evidence that was in front of him.

As Suzie watched the police officers begin to leave, and Warren's body was whisked away to the medical examiner's office, she wished she could force them to stay. She was certain that they were missing something important. Mary walked over to her as the last police car pulled out of the parking lot.

"Where is everyone going?" she asked with concern.

"They don't believe me," Suzie said impatiently. "Not even Jason or Kirk."

"It's okay, Suzie, try not to let it get to you," Mary said soothingly.

“I'm not going to let it get to me,” Suzie said sternly. “I'm going to solve this murder myself if they won't do it.”

“No, you are not,” Mary shot back just as sternly.

“What are you saying, Mary?” Suzie asked incredulously. “Do you really just expect me to allow someone to be killed at Dune House without getting to the bottom of it?”

“Of course not,” Mary shook her head. “But you will not be solving this crime, we will be solving this crime,” she looked into her friend's eyes. “You're not alone in this, Suzie.”

Mary's words caused a warm smile to rise to Suzie's lips. “Thank you, Mary,” she said.

“Where do we start?” Mary asked as she swept her gaze over the towering form of Dune House. In the pale light of dawn it looked more like a ghost than a beautiful, old building.

“We need to inspect the balcony, and Warren's room,” Suzie said.

"Then let's get started."

Chapter Five

Suzie and Mary began walking towards Dune house. “If we believe that this wasn't an accident then we need to think about who would have done this to Warren and why,” Mary pointed out. “There's got to be a reason this happened. It seems to have been obviously orchestrated not just some random event.”

“You're right,” Suzie said as she held open the door for Mary. “I saw this car lingering around the house earlier this evening. I tried to tell Jason about it, but I don't think that he listened. It's possible that the car had something to do with Warren’s death, especially if he was murdered.”

“The important thing is that we know that it wasn't our fault,” Mary said as they walked up the stairs towards the room that Warren had been staying in.

“That won't make much of a difference when we get hit with a lawsuit,” Suzie pointed out gravely. "We need real evidence, real proof that this was not an accident. That's not even the worst part. The worst part is that there won't be any justice for Warren's death. I know that he was killed, and yet his death will be ruled an accident. His friends and loved ones will never get the proper closure that they deserve. I hate to think that all of this could happen under our roof."

"I know," Mary nodded when they reached the landing of the third floor. "All we can do is hope that the autopsy turns up some evidence. Maybe, we'll find something while we're looking around the room, but I doubt the police will have missed anything. You know that Jason usually does a very thorough job, and his new partner, Kirk, seems to pay keen attention to detail."

"Don't be so sure," Suzie said. "If they made the assumption that it was an accident then they could have very easily overlooked some important evidence. Assuming things can make you blind."

"Not Jason though," Mary pointed out. "He's very observant, and very good at his job and Kirk seems to be as well."

"Maybe so, but as far as I'm concerned he jumped to the same incorrect conclusion that the rest of the police officers did, so we can't rely on him finding any evidence," she frowned as she recalled the way that she had spoken to him. "I think I might have upset him," she added quietly.

"You were upset, Suzie," Mary said with a slight shake of her head. "In the heat of the moment we all say things that we don't really mean."

"But I shouldn't have said it," Suzie sighed as they reached the room that Warren had been staying in. The police had sealed off the door so no one could get in. Suzie pushed the tape aside and opened the door with her key. "Sometimes I forget that Jason and I are just about the only family we both have. I'd hate to alienate him because of a little squabble."

"I think Jason is sturdier than that," Mary assured her. "Trust me, my kids and I had plenty of arguments, and each one made me worry. Would they ever speak to me again? Would they hold it against me forever? But life happens, people forgive, and we all move on. It's going to be fine, Suzie, I promise."

Suzie felt a little better. Mary always had wisdom to share, especially when it came to dealing with the younger generation. Suzie was a little too impatient to try to look at things from their perspective, but Mary always took the time to look at things through the eyes of others. Hopefully that would help them find some real evidence about what had happened to Warren.

"Jason was right, not a thing is out of place," Suzie said grimly as she looked around the room. She ducked her head into the bathroom. All of the towels were hanging perfectly. There was nothing missing. When she stepped back into the room, Mary was studying the bed.

"It looks like he might have just got up," Mary said as she pointed to the way the blankets were shoved aside. "It looks as if he got up quickly. It doesn't look like he had been watching television. The remote for the television is over here," she pointed to the bureau the television was sitting on. "Maybe he was sleeping and something woke him, something startled him."

"Yes, so why did he get up and go onto the balcony?" Suzie asked thoughtfully as she looked around the room for an explanation.

"Maybe he had a nightmare," Mary suggested and tapped her chin lightly. "Maybe he had a phone call that woke him."

"I can check the call logs to the room," Suzie said with a slow nod. "I'm sure Jason has taken his cell phone and wallet so that he can make next of kin notifications. We won't be able to tell if he had a call at that time. Hopefully, Jason will at least check that."

"Well, he didn't take this," Mary said as she slid something out from under the bed. It was a soft-sided leather briefcase.

"See what I mean?" Suzie said with

annoyance. “If they had done a thorough search they would have found that underneath the bed. Instead it is here for us to find.”

“Maybe, but what matters is we found it,” Mary said with some excitement. “Maybe there's something in here that could tell us why someone would want to kill him. Maybe he had been involved in some criminal behavior, or he had recently made someone angry enough for them to want him dead.”

“Do you think the murder could have something to do with Louis' rare book?” Suzie suggested curiously.

“Maybe,” Mary shrugged. “But what could it have to do with it? Louis has the book at his house. Warren didn't even have it yet. So, why would he be killed over it?”

“Good point,” Suzie nodded and stepped up beside her.

“Let's see what is in here,” Mary said.

She set the briefcase down on the bed and

popped it open. Inside were a few file folders, a deck of cards, and a few packs of gum.

"Looks like the folders are for different clients," Mary said. "Here is Louis'."

She set the folder down on the bed beside the briefcase. Suzie picked it up and flipped it open. Inside were the photographs of the book that Louis had sent to Warren before Warren had agreed to come out to value it. Warren had made a few notes on the white frame around the photographs.

"The book looks authentic. If it is it will be worth a lot. I have some concern about the binding," Suzie read aloud as she turned the picture.

"What concern do you think he had about the binding?" Mary asked suspiciously.

"He seemed to have circled the thread," Suzie said as she pointed to a mark on the picture.

"Hmm," Mary said as she studied the picture. "I wonder why he circled it."

"No idea," Suzie sighed.

"Well, then I guess we're back to square one," Mary said with a light cluck of her tongue.

"Okay, let's forget about the book for the moment," Suzie said. "Let's walk through what his last moments were like," she cringed at saying those words. It was still hard for her to believe that Warren was actually gone.

"Okay, well we know that he was likely asleep," Mary said.

Suzie walked over to the bed and stood beside it. "Which means that it would have been dark," she said and pointed to the light switch. "Turn off the light please, Mary," she said. Mary walked over to the light switch and flipped it off. The room was plunged into darkness, but for the dawn's light that was beginning to filter in through the sliding glass doors that led out onto the balcony. "Okay, so he wakes up," Suzie said with a frown. "We don't know what woke him, but let's presume that it made him jump up out of bed," she said and walked to the end of the bed. "It's dark. Does he go over and turn the light on?" Suzie asked.

"When I came up here the light was off," Mary said. "I turned it on when I walked into the room."

"Wait a minute," Suzie said and narrowed her eyes. "Was the door locked?"

"Yes, I had the master key with me," Mary said. "I grabbed it when I heard the scream. It sounded like it was coming from this room, so after knocking and calling out when I received no answer, I unlocked and opened the door and stepped inside. It was dark, I called out again and I still heard no answer. I flipped the light on," she said.

"Okay, so when he got up out of bed, he didn't bother to turn the light on," Suzie said with a grim frown. "If I hear something that startles me, one of the first things I do is switch on a light," Suzie pointed out.

"Me, too," Mary nodded.

“So, either he knew what the sound was, or he was so startled by it that he didn't feel he could take the time to turn the light on,” Suzie explained. “If the door was locked, then it's not likely someone was in the room with him. So, how could he have been shoved off the balcony?” she frowned and shook her head.

“Wait, you're getting ahead of yourself,” Mary warned as she stepped closer to Suzie. “He's up, he hears something, maybe sees something, but more than likely hears it since it is dark. He doesn't turn the light on, he wants to know what that noise is. No one is in the room with him. He must think it's coming from outside, right?” Mary said as she walked towards the sliding glass doors.

“Okay, so whatever he hears, is coming from outside,” Suzie said softly. “That would explain why he wouldn't turn the light on. Maybe he was frightened and didn't want to reveal that he was awake.”

“What could he hear from outside that would cause him to be frightened though?” Mary asked with a frown. “Remember, it couldn't have been too loud, or we would have heard it, too.”

Suzie and Mary stood in silence for a few minutes. Suzie kept thinking about what would cause her to be startled and even frightened if she woke up to the sound of it. Suddenly her heart dropped.

“Knocking,” she said in a whisper. “He must have heard knocking, on the sliding glass doors.”

“Oh yes!” Mary nodded. “That would have made him jump up out of bed. He would have been afraid to turn the light on, and he would have crept outside to see what the noise was.”

“Okay, so he decides he's going to look outside, which means that whatever was causing the sound was not something that he could see through the doors. He opens the door,” she said as she slid the glass door open. She gazed out at the dangling railing where there was more tape that the police had put there to warn people that it was unsafe. “He steps outside.”

"Be careful, Suzie!" Mary said as Suzie stepped out onto the balcony.

"I am," Suzie promised her. "He's outside and, then what?" Suzie asked, puzzled.

"If there was someone knocking then they might have been waiting for him on the balcony," Mary suggested. "Maybe when he stepped out, the person shoved him hard enough to break the railing."

Suzie frowned. "That makes sense, but it can't be true," she said.

"Why not?" Mary asked with confusion.

"Jason said there was no damage to the railing, no sign of it being broken. Instead it looks like it just came loose," she shook her head. "But you and I both know that there is no way the balcony came loose."

"Okay," Mary murmured thoughtfully.

"Besides, even if the murderer was up here with Warren, where did he go?" Suzie asked. "Not to be morbid, but how long do you think it could have taken for Warren to fall from the balcony to the ground?"

"Not long," Mary grimaced.

"About as long as the scream we heard," Suzie pointed out. "You went upstairs, I went outside. How could the killer have had time to escape if we were covering both ways to exit?"

"Good point," Mary nodded as she glanced around the balcony. "Even if he had a rope attached to the balcony, we would have found the rope."

"It's too far to jump," Suzie pointed out.

"Unbelievable," Mary sighed. "It's no wonder Jason thought this was an accident. It's nearly impossible to prove otherwise."

"But it wasn't an accident," Suzie reminded her sternly. She just hoped that she was right. "So, there must be something here that we're overlooking. So, what is it?" Suzie mused as she stood in the middle of the balcony. It seemed very sturdy despite the railing being broken. It was still anchored to the side of the house. It was designed not to collapse even in the highest winds. Suzie felt secure standing on it. "If the killer was not on the balcony, what did Warren see when he stepped out here?" she frowned.

"From the way he landed I think it's very likely that he was leaning on the railing," Mary pointed out as she stepped out onto the balcony as well.

"So, he was too frightened to turn the light on," Suzie said as she looked back into the dark room. "But something prompted him to step all the way out onto the balcony, and lean on the railing."

Suzie walked towards the edge of the balcony where the railing and wooden slats swung free from the base of the balcony.

"Suzie, be careful!" Mary said gravely. "That is a long way down."

"I know it is," Suzie agreed and stopped about a foot away from the edge of the balcony. "So,

Warren walked over to the railing after seeing that no one was on the balcony. Maybe he continued to hear something. Maybe he could tell that now it was coming from below him."

"That would make him lean against the railing in order to look over the side," Mary said with a slight nod. "So, whoever did this, was still trying to coax him out to the edge of the balcony even if they weren't on the balcony waiting for him."

"And because they weren't on the balcony, there is no evidence left behind," Suzie said with a deep sigh. "There's not going to be any physical evidence of the killer up here, because he might not have ever been up here."

"He let the balcony do his work for him," Mary said. She cringed. "Which also gives the killer a clear cover for the murder, because it sure does look like the only possibility is an accident due to a weak railing."

"Who in the world would go to this much trouble?" Suzie asked with disbelief. "We still don't know how the killer lured Warren out here, or why."

"No, we don't," Mary agreed. "But we do suspect that he was lured. So, someone likely waited until he thought we would all be asleep. He wanted this done at a time that no one could possibly stop it, or catch him."

"If I wasn't awake, it might have taken me even longer to get out there," Suzie said grimly.

"What about our other guest?" Mary asked. "Do you think we should check on him?"

"I think if he slept through the sirens and the commotion then he deserves a good night's sleep," Suzie said with a sigh. "I'll explain everything to him in the morning."

"It is the morning," Mary pointed out as she looked out over the water. The colors of the sunrise were spilling out across the calm slate of the water. It seemed as if the waves had hushed in reverence to the transition from night into day.

"It's beautiful," Suzie said solemnly as Mary

came to stand beside her. Even though something horrible had happened just a little while before, the view from Dune House was still too stunning for words.

"Maybe we should try to get a little rest," Mary suggested.

"Not yet," Suzie said. "I want to make sure that I've scoured every inch of this balcony first."

"Okay," Mary nodded and swept her gaze over the balcony. "There isn't much to see though."

"We must be missing something," Suzie said under her breath.

Suzie crouched down and studied the floorboards of the balcony. She could see where there was some scuffing from shoes, but there was no actual damage to the wood. She knew that the balcony was in very good shape. She wasn't sure what she was looking for. She was hoping that there might be some hint of what happened carved into the wood. As she neared the edge of the balcony the only thing she noticed were some pistachio shells. She narrowed her eyes at the sight of them.

"Well, that's a little odd," Suzie said to herself.

"What is?" Mary asked when she overheard her comment.

"There are pistachio shells over here," Suzie explained and picked one up. It looked fresh enough to have been tossed in the last few days, but Warren was the only one she had rented that room to, and that was only because of the antiques that she had decorated the room with.

"So, he was snacking?" Mary asked with a frown. "Maybe he had them earlier, but if he had them just before he fell off the balcony I guess that throws a wrench in our theory about him being frightened."

"It doesn't make sense," Suzie agreed and dropped the pistachio shell. "I don't know, Mary, maybe we're thinking about this all wrong. What if he knew that there would be someone outside?"

"Like a meeting he had planned with

someone?" Mary suggested.

"Sure. Maybe he had set an alarm to wake up at a certain time. He didn't turn the light on, because he didn't want to alert any of us that he was awake. Then he went out on the balcony to wait, with his pistachios," she shrugged.

"I don't know, if he had a meeting, why would he be on the balcony?" Mary pointed out. "Why wouldn't he have met them downstairs where he could have spoken to them more directly?"

"Who knows," Suzie sighed. "I don't think this investigation is getting us anywhere."

"Let's take another look inside," Mary suggested. "There still might be something we're not thinking about."

"Okay," Suzie nodded, but her shoulders had slumped with defeat. She didn't want to admit it out loud but she could see why Jason had found it hard to believe that this death wasn't an accident. Everything about the scene pointed to an accident. Maybe it was just an accident after all and she just didn't want to admit that they had a faulty railing. Suzie tried to push that thought from her mind, probably because she simply didn't want to believe it.

Suzie stepped back into the room with Mary just behind her. When she slid the door shut, she noticed a strange spattering of marks on the glass. The morning sunlight filtering through the glass made it very easy to see. They didn't look like fingerprints.

"I wonder what caused this," Suzie said as she studied the marks. "I know they weren't here before Warren checked in. I did a thorough cleaning."

"Sometimes you can't get all of the smudges," Mary pointed out. "Sunlight can be very unforgiving."

"I guess that you're right," Suzie nodded. She ducked down to look under the bed again. Then she picked up a few of the pillows to see if there was anything hidden underneath. She found nothing unusual. She picked up the trashcan which only had a few papers in it. One was a receipt from a restaurant on the way to Dune House. Suzie remembered that he had said he ate on the road. Another paper was a scribble of what looked like one of the antique vases that lined the shelving. The last piece of paper was crumpled up. Suzie thought it might be very important. If he had taken the time to wad it up into a ball he probably didn't want anyone easily seeing what was written on it.

"I think we've got something, Mary," Suzie said. She carefully unfolded the paper.

"Oh yes, you have something all right," Mary gulped out and cringed at the sight of the used chewing gum that Suzie had unveiled.

"Gross," Suzie cringed and wadded the paper back up. "That's it then," she said with a huff. "There's nothing. There's not even a bag of leftover pistachios around here."

"We should have a look around down below

the balcony, too," Mary suggested.

"Good idea," Suzie nodded. She walked back across the room to lock the doors that led to the balcony. She didn't want there to be any chance of anyone else getting hurt. When she turned back to leave the room, she saw the mirror positioned on the bed across from the sliding glass doors. In the mirror she could see the sun rising, the water glistening, and the balcony railing swinging. Her heart skipped a beat as she wondered just for a second if somehow Warren's death really was her fault. As she stared through the mirror she noticed the smudges on the glass door again. She was certain they hadn't been there when Warren checked in. With a shake of her head she left the room. She locked the door behind her.

"Are you okay?" Mary asked when Suzie joined her in the hallway.

"I don't think I will be until we find out what happened," Suzie admitted. She felt a heavy weight on her shoulders. She knew that she still had a birthday party to plan. Benjamin and

Catherine would still be flying in, and they would expect to be able to celebrate with their mother. Suzie had to find a way to juggle everything, and she still wanted it to be a surprise for Mary. As they walked down the stairs to the lobby, Suzie noticed John standing by the front desk. He looked a little uncomfortable. Suzie assumed he had seen some of what happened.

"Sorry for all of the commotion," Suzie said sadly as she walked over to the desk.

"I'll make some coffee," Mary offered and headed for the kitchen. Suzie was sure that she was going to need some to get through the rest of the day.

"What happened?" John asked. "I woke up and saw a bunch of police cars driving off. Was there a break-in?"

"Not exactly," Suzie stared at him for a moment. She had no idea what to tell him. A man had died. She considered it murder, the police considered it an accident, but John was looking at her expectantly as he waited for an explanation. "To be honest we're not exactly sure what happened yet," Suzie said finally. She expected that John would question her further, but he only nodded.

"Well, I need to head off today, so I just wanted to check-out," he explained. Suzie pulled up the billing program on the computer.

"Of course. There is nothing outstanding as you paid already for the room and didn't have any meals."

"Great," he nodded and handed her the key.

"Thank you for staying with us, John. I hope that you will consider Dune House as an option for future travel."

"I will," he nodded a little. Then he turned and hurried out the door. Suzie watched him leave. She thought he was a little odd, but then she was used to many of her guests being unique.

Chapter Six

"Coffee," Mary said as she walked into the lobby with two cups.

"Excellent," Suzie said and took the coffee mug from her. "Thank you."

"Did the other guest leave?" she asked as she leaned against the desk and took a sip of her coffee.

"Yes," Suzie said with a frown. "I don't think he heard anything that happened, he just saw the police cars as they were leaving."

"Suzie, I know you don't want to think about it, but news of this death is going to get around Garber really fast," Mary said hesitantly. "I hate to say it, but we might have to think about how we are going to counter the rumors. It's not going to look too good for Dune House if people are talking about a fatal accident."

"I know," Suzie admitted grimly. "I was

hoping to prove that it wasn't an accident, but it looks like that will be much harder than I initially thought. All we can do at this point is hope our good reputation will stand up against the gossip."

"Too bad we haven't even been open a year," Mary pointed out. "We don't even know everyone in town all that well. Don't you think they will be quick to blame this on us?"

"I'm sure they will be," Suzie set down her coffee mug. "But we can't control what people say. All we can do is try our best to find out the truth. I can't worry about business when there's a man who has lost his life, with no one looking for his murderer."

"No one but us," Mary pointed out. "Maybe I'll try giving Wes a call. I could see if he would check out that car you mentioned. If Jason won't do it, or can't, then maybe Wes will."

"You wouldn't mind calling him?" Suzie asked. "After the way that he treated you last night?"

"I had a little time to cool down," Mary admitted. "I really think that maybe I was being a little too sensitive about things."

"Birthdays can do that to people," Suzie reminded her. "But I don't think that you were out of line for how you felt. He left you in the middle of dinner, and didn't even bother to drive you home himself. I was so mad that I..." she stopped suddenly.

"That you what?" Mary demanded as she met Suzie's eyes. "Suzie, what did you do?"

"Nothing too serious," Suzie said with a grimace. "It's not like I egged his car or anything. I just called him to give him a piece of my mind."

"Suzie, you didn't!" Mary gasped, horrified by the idea.

"Well, no I didn't," Suzie frowned. "I was sent to voicemail."

Mary sighed with relief. "Suzie, I know that you're only trying to help me, but I really don't want you getting in the middle of this. What is between Wes and me is between Wes and me. Okay?"

Suzie frowned. "I don't know if I can promise that Mary. I just don't want him to hurt you."

"I can take care of myself, Suzie," Mary stated.

"Of course you can," Suzie blushed. "I just get so angry when someone does something to hurt you, Mary. You mean the world to me, and you're always doing things for others. I just want to see your kindness rewarded, not taken advantage of."

"I understand, Suzie," Mary smiled warmly. "But you have to remember, I'm a big girl. I can take care of myself. I would like to be able to handle this on my own. So promise me that you will stay out of it, please?"

Suzie grumbled a little. She stalled by taking a sip of her coffee. The last thing that she wanted to do was agree to what Mary was asking. Suzie wanted to protect Mary if she felt the need to. But Mary continued to stare straight at her, offering her no option to get out of the promise.

"Fine," Suzie finally agreed reluctantly. "I will stay out of it, unless you say otherwise."

"Thank you, Suzie," Mary said. She leaned across the desk and hugged her friend. "I'll go call Wes," she said as she headed off to her room. Suzie was still in her robe. She knew she needed to get dressed. Her mind was spinning as she walked towards her room. She had no idea how to explain Warren's death, she simply knew that it wasn't an accident. She set her coffee mug down on her bedside table and walked over to her closet to pull out some clothes. While she was dressing she remembered that she was supposed to meet Paul for dinner that night. Once dressed she sat down on the edge of her bed and picked up her phone. If he didn't know about the death yet, he would know soon enough. She wanted him to hear it from her first. She could only hope that he wouldn't share Jason's opinion. He answered on the third ring.

"Hello?" he asked with a bit of heaviness in his voice. Suzie realized it was still quite early and he had likely been sleeping.

"Sorry to wake you," Suzie said softly.

"Don't be sorry, your voice is the best sound I could wake up to," Paul said warmly. Suzie smiled a little despite her worry.

"A guest died here early this morning," Suzie said quickly. There was no easy way to break the news.

"Huh? Wow," he said. "How did that happen? A medical issue?"

"No," Suzie frowned. "He was killed."

"Killed?" Paul nearly roared. "Where are you? Did they catch the killer?"

"I'm at home, at Dune House," Suzie explained. "No one is even looking for the killer. Jason believes that it was an accident."

"Maybe you could start from the beginning and explain all of this to me?" Paul asked. "I know you must be upset."

"I am," Suzie admitted and began to tear up.

"I talked with the man last night, he was very nice. I had no idea that something like this would have happened."

"How could you know?" Paul asked grimly.

"Early this morning, before the sun came up, I heard a scream. The guest, Warren, had fallen from the balcony on the third floor. I found him on the sand below, he was already gone," she explained.

"So, it was an accident?" he asked with confusion.

"No," Suzie said firmly. "There's no way it could have been an accident. The railing was secure, it wouldn't have just given way."

Paul was silent on the other end of the phone for a moment. "Well, it's not likely," he agreed. "Did the police find anything to indicate foul play?"

"No," Suzie sighed. "Mary and I searched the balcony as well. The only thing suspicious was that car I told you about yesterday, remember?"

"I remember," Paul said gravely. "I wouldn't read too much into that though, Suzie. You know that it could have just been someone having a look."

"I know that," Suzie said impatiently. "I also know that there is no way this was an accident."

"Hey, slow down, Suzie," Paul said firmly. "You don't have to convince me. I'm on your side, love, if you say it wasn't an accident, it wasn't an accident."

Suzie smiled with relief at his words. "Thanks Paul, I needed to hear that."

"I just hope you and Mary are careful. If there is someone on the loose that caused this man to die, then you need to be extra cautious, in case he intends to come back," Paul pointed out.

"I don't think they'll be back," Suzie said grimly. "We were all vulnerable last night, but Warren was obviously targeted. There's no reason why someone would go to all the trouble of attacking someone on the third floor unless they intended him to be the victim."

"I'm sure the police will figure this out," Paul said carefully.

"They're calling it an accident, Paul, I don't think that they'll even investigate it," she muttered.

"Jason's a good police officer, Suzie, he'll figure it out," he assured her. "Do you want me to come over?"

"No, that's okay," Suzie sighed. "I'm going to do some cleaning around here and prepare some things for the party."

"You're still having it?" he asked.

"Yes, Benjamin and Catherine already have their plane tickets, and I've already paid for the cake and catering. I don't want to cancel it now," she explained.

"Okay," he agreed. "Does that mean we're still on for tonight?" he asked hopefully.

Suzie thought about it for a moment. She

wasn't sure if she could enjoy a dinner date with all of this on her mind. But it would be her last chance to see Paul before he shipped out. She didn't want to miss out on that.

"Yes," she finally said.

"Good," he said with relief. "I can't imagine launching without getting to spend a little time with you first. I'll pick you up around five?"

"Perfect," Suzie replied. She just hoped that she would be in a better mood by then. After hanging up the phone she took a moment to sit on the side of the bed. What had happened was a lot to process. How to deal with it, was even more difficult. She wasn't sure how she could just go on about her day. Sure, there were things to do for the party, and there were things to do to defend Dune House against potential lawsuits, but all she could think of was Warren sprawled across the sand. Her mind was stuck on how that could have happened.

She could have kicked herself for not

questioning John, the guest who had just checked out, more thoroughly. Maybe he had noticed something, maybe he had heard something that could have given her a clue. Suzie doubted it, but it still would have been better if she had asked. She knew that Jason would be handling notifying the next of kin, but she wondered if anyone had notified Louis yet. She walked towards the kitchen. Mary was leaning against the counter, staring aimlessly at a bagel that had popped up out of the toaster.

"Did you talk to Wes?" Suzie asked as she plucked the bagel out of the toaster. "Butter or cream cheese?" she asked.

"Jelly," Mary replied, still in a bit of a daze.

"Jelly, are you sure?" Suzie asked with surprise. "You never want jelly on your bagel."

"I'm trying out something new," Mary explained and then blinked a few times. "Yes, I spoke with Wes," she added.

"How did that go?" Suzie asked and cast a

sidelong glance in her direction.

"Well, let's just say that he was very apologetic," Mary replied with a grimace. "I just don't think he realized how rude it was to run out on me like that. Of course he didn't really explain why he took off."

"At least he is aware of the error of his ways," Suzie pointed out. She spread a healthy helping of grape jelly across each side of the toasted bagel.

"Yes, that's true," Mary nodded. "When I told him what happened, he was pretty upset."

"Did he believe you when you told him that it wasn't an accident?" Suzie asked. "That's the important question."

"I don't know to be honest," Mary sighed. "I kept insisting that the railing was sound, and he kept insisting that if it wasn't, the fault should be placed on the company that we hired to update the balconies."

"So, he just talked around it," Suzie asked with a grim frown. "I didn't expect much different from him."

"Well, it doesn't matter what he, or Jason thinks, we know the truth, Suzie," Mary said firmly.

"Here's your bagel," Suzie said and handed her the plate. "Did you mention the car that I saw to Wes?"

"Thank you," Mary said with a warm smile. "I did mention it to him. He said that he would look into it, but just a color and description isn't much to go on."

"Great," Suzie sighed. "Well, at least he is going to look into it. I think I'm going to call Louis and see if anyone has contacted him about this."

"About what?" Louis said from the front door. Suzie realized she had left the exterior door open when she came back inside.

"Louis," Suzie said, her heart pounding faster.

"Is Warren up yet?" he asked. "I was going to take him to breakfast. No offense against your cooking, Mary, I just thought it would be a courteous thing to do."

Mary grimaced and set down her plate. "I don't think that is going to be possible, Louis," she said gingerly.

Suzie braced herself. She walked towards Louis, who looked a little confused. "Unfortunately, Louis, Warren died early this morning," she said matter-of-factly. She believed in ripping the band-aid off quickly, especially when it came to news like this.

"What?" Louis' eyes widened. "Are you playing some kind of prank on me?"

"No, Louis," Mary said in a soothing tone. "We're telling you the truth. Warren died early this morning, his body is at the medical examiner's office."

"What? Why?" Louis asked and grasped the kitchen counter to hold himself up. He had gone very pale. "How did this happen?" he demanded.

"He fell from the balcony," Suzie explained haltingly. "Well, we believe he was killed, the police believe it was an accident."

"If I had known that it wasn't safe here..." Louis gasped out.

"Louis, please," Mary said. "You know how careful we have been with restorations. We didn't cause this to happen."

"You said you think he was killed, why do you think that?" Louis asked desperately.

"Because I don't believe that the railing could have given way that easily," Suzie said with confidence. "What happened is a tragedy, but I do not believe that it was an accident."

"Does it matter?" Louis asked in a whisper. "Whether he was killed or it was an accident, he's gone. Because of me."

"It's certainly not because of you," Mary said swiftly. "You couldn't have known any of this would happen."

"But he never would have been here if it wasn't to evaluate my book," Louis pointed out tearfully.

“Louis, it's going to be okay,” Suzie said and wrapped an arm around his shoulders. “I know this is quite a shock, but it is going to be okay.”

“I hope so,” he murmured. “I guess I should go. I should probably call Gerald. I don't know.”

“Have some coffee, Louis,” Mary said. “Take a seat, and drink some coffee. It'll help you settle down.”

“I don't think I should,” Louis sighed. “I was so excited about Warren's visit that I didn't sleep at all last night. If I drink coffee I'll be wired.”

“Maybe it's best if you do go home and get some rest then,” Suzie suggested.

“I think that would be best,” Louis agreed. He looked between the two women. “I'm sorry for what I said. I didn't mean to accuse you of anything.”

“It's okay,” Mary said. “I'll walk you out.”

“Thanks,” Louis nodded. As Mary walked him out of Dune House, Suzie frowned. She knew that Louis was just the beginning. Everyone in Garber would soon believe that a fatal accident had occurred at Dune House.

"I think I'm going to lay down for a little while," Mary said when she walked back inside. "I don't know if I'll be able to sleep, but I need to get off of my knees."

"I understand," Suzie nodded. "I'm going to see if I can persuade Jason to take another look at this situation."

"Good luck," Mary said. "Wake me if I can do anything to help."

"Get some good sleep," Suzie said as she pulled out her cell phone. While Mary walked down the hallway to her room, Suzie dialed Jason's number.

"Hi Suzie," Jason said when he picked up on the first ring.

"I just wanted to check in with you, Jason, and apologize for the way I spoke to you earlier," Suzie added.

"No need," he replied calmly. "I know

emotions run high when something like this happens."

"That's true, Jason. But I want you to think about the possibility that maybe I was right. Maybe there is something more to all of this than you can see on the surface," she pressed.

"Oh, Suzie you're not still on this murder idea are you?" he asked grimly.

"I am," she replied. "Because I know that it is true. Warren Blasser was murdered. How can you not even want to look into it?"

"It isn't about what I want, Suzie," Jason said in a colder tone. "This is my job here. I can't look like a fool to everyone around me just because you have a hunch."

"It's more than a hunch, Jason," Suzie sighed and pressed the phone tighter to her ear. "Listen to me. I had those railings and the balconies updated and inspected. I wouldn't lie to you about that, Jason. I know that we're still getting to know each other, but if I thought it was possible that this was an accident I would admit to it."

"I know that, Suzie," he said gently. "I don't want you to think I don't believe you. I know that you believe that this could not have been an accident. Don't think I'm not looking at that angle, it's just that right now there is absolutely nothing to point to foul play. Maybe when the results come back from the autopsy tomorrow, we'll get a better idea of what really happened. Until then, I think you should just do your best to prepare for what those results might be."

"I'll try," Suzie said. "I appreciate you listening to me, Jason."

"Suzie, you know how much I respect you. Just give me some time to see if anything suspicious comes up," he said.

"Okay," she agreed. "Thank you, Jason." When she hung up the phone, she felt a little better. Knowing that Jason wasn't completely opposed to the idea that there had been a murder, she could relax a little. She glanced at her watch and saw that she had a few hours before Paul would arrive. She decided she would take a nap as well, even though she had a million other things that she needed to do. She didn't realize how exhausted she was until she curled up in her bed.

Chapter Seven

The ringing of Suzie's cell phone woke her from a deep sleep. She felt like she had just closed her eyes. But when she grabbed her phone she could see that it was after five. It was Paul who was calling.

"Suzie, I'm here," he said when she answered the phone.

"I'm sorry, Paul, I fell asleep," she mumbled and pulled herself out of bed. "Give me a second." She quickly got ready and then made her way down the hallway to the front door of Dune House. She unlocked the door and opened it for Paul.

"Oh sweetheart, I didn't mean to wake you," he said quietly.

"It's good that you did," Suzie said with a laugh. "Apparently, I was going to sleep for hours."

"If you're not up for dinner it's okay, Suzie," Paul said and gave her a soft hug.

"Are you kidding?" Suzie shook her head. "I'm starving."

"Great," he smiled. "What about Mary? Is she all right?"

"She's sleeping, too," Suzie said. "It's probably best if we let her rest."

"Do you need a few minutes before we go?" Paul asked. Suzie brushed her fingers back through her brassy blonde hair and shook her head.

"I'm fine, if you're ready," she said. She suddenly had a deep desire to get away from Dune House.

"Sounds good," he agreed. He led her across the deck and to the parking lot. Suzie searched the parking lot for any sign of the mustard colored car she had seen the night before. There wasn't a hint of it. In fact the only cars in the parking lot were the car that Suzie and Mary shared and Paul's. He opened the passenger door for her. Suzie slid inside and did her best to relax. She tried to convince herself that there was nothing she could do at the moment. She tried to give herself permission to actually enjoy her time with Paul.

When Suzie and Paul reached their favorite restaurant, Cheney's, Suzie was still trying to convince herself. She realized she hadn't spoken a word to Paul. Paul, who was usually rather quiet himself hadn't tried to coax her into conversation, but she knew that he had noticed. They walked up to the restaurant, hand in hand, but Suzie's mind was elsewhere.

"I'm sorry all of this happened, and especially on Mary's birthday weekend," Paul said grimly.

"Me too," Suzie said as he held the door open for her. There was a subtle buzz of conversation when they stepped inside, but as soon as the door fell closed behind them, that buzz became stony silence. Suzie was a little confused until she noticed people leaning close to whisper to each other. The hostess offered her a sad smile. Suzie felt a sense of alarm growing within her that she hadn't felt since she was in high school and had been teased for the braces she had to wear. She wasn't sure how to react to the knowledge that everyone in the room was talking about her. She felt Paul's strong hand on the small of her back.

"Table for two," he told the hostess.

"Paul, maybe we should just get the food to go," Suzie said softly beside his ear.

"Nonsense," he replied. "I'm going to take any chance I have to show you off."

Suzie raised an eyebrow at that. "I don't think that anyone wants me to be here," she said.

"I do," he said and met her eyes intently. "It's just you and me, sweetheart, nobody else here matters."

Suzie realized he was trying to prevent her from running and hiding, but she wasn't so sure she agreed with him. She did her best to make it through the meal without bolting out the door, but she had a hard time thinking about anything other than the dirty looks, and curious stares she continued to receive. Obviously the rumor had spread through the majority of the town. Now, people were likely debating whether the death was the fault of Dune House and its owner.

Paul signaled to the waitress to bring their bill. Suzie felt a sense of relief. She couldn't even enjoy her food as her stomach was in knots. While they waited for the bill Suzie did something she almost never did. She pulled out her cell phone at the table. She texted Jason to see if he had found out anything about the case. She also sent a text to Mary to check on her. She wanted to do anything to avoid noticing the people around her who were judging her.

"Why don't we go for a walk?" Paul suggested. "It's a nice night for it."

"I'd like that," Suzie said and finally put her phone away.

As they left the restaurant Suzie could feel the eyes of others on her. She wasn't sure if she was just being paranoid, or if there really was something for her to be suspicious about. Either way she imagined that they were thinking horrible things about her. She was hoping that a little fresh air and escape from the people of Garber would help clear her mind. Paul led her down towards the harbor where his boat was docked.

"You seem a little preoccupied," Paul said quietly as they walked hand in hand.

"I'm sorry," Suzie said with a slight frown as she looked over at him. "Between this situation with Dune House, and Mary, I am a little preoccupied."

"The party?" he asked and raised an eyebrow. "Do you need help with it?"

"No, it's not the party," Suzie sighed. "I've barely even thought about the party since all of this happened. It's Wes."

"Detective Brown?" Paul said with a grimace.

"I know you're not a fan," Suzie shook her head. "Maybe I should have listened to you."

"Now, I may not be a fan, but he's turned out to be a decent guy," Paul shrugged a little. "I don't think he'd do anything to hurt Mary."

"Well, he seems to be up to something, and it's really getting to Mary," Suzie explained. "I just wish I could fix it for her. With her birthday coming up, it's not a great time for her to be worrying about romance."

"That's true," Paul said and wrapped his arm around her waist. "But you can't make people do what you want, I've tried," he said thoughtfully. "As hard as it might be you're going to have to let things play out between Mary and Wes."

"I know," she frowned. "I just have a hard time watching her get hurt."

"Of course you do," he leaned close and kissed her cheek. "It's never easy. But keep in mind, sometimes things are not how they look on the surface."

"I think Mary's spent enough years dealing with a man who played games with her," Suzie said darkly. “She deserves more than that. She deserves to be happy.”

“And you know as well as I do, that another person can't do that for you,” Paul reminded her wisely. He paused in the moonlight, and drew her close. “She is a lucky woman, Suzie, she has you in her life to love and protect her.”

“I guess,” Suzie shook her head. “But now with the possibility of us being sued, what happens if we lose Dune House, where will that leave her? She has nowhere else to turn. Her kids are in college, her ex-husband took the house and the savings...”

“Take a breath,” Paul advised and looked into her eyes. “Sometimes you just have to have faith that it will all work out.”

“Faith?” she looked at him with surprise. “You're one of the biggest cynics I know, Paul.”

“Thanks, I think,” he said with a half-smile. “That is true, but I learned that having a little faith can make a big difference.”

"How?" she asked curiously.

"When I fell in love with you," he explained as he held her gaze, "I wanted to make you see just how good we could be together, but I couldn't do that. You didn't want to see it. I just had to have faith that you would feel the same way I did, and now look where we are."

"True," Suzie said hesitantly. "I didn't think you were ever going to last."

"Thanks a lot," Paul said with a laugh and leaned in for a quick kiss. When he pulled away he was smiling. "I guess I had faith enough for both of us."

"So, what you're saying is I need to stay out of it," Suzie said grimly. "I'm not too great about keeping my nose out of things."

"Not necessarily stay out of it, but take a step back and let things play out as they will. Mary needs to figure things out for herself. You and I both believe that railing was tampered with. The proof will come to light with time," he studied her intently. “I don't want to go off to sea worried about what you might be getting in the middle of, Suzie. If someone really did murder Warren Blasser, then that person is dangerous.”

“This isn't going to be one of those lectures about me not putting myself in danger is it?” Suzie asked with a subtle sigh of impatience.

“Maybe,” Paul admitted. He shrugged and swept his gaze over the water before looking back at her. “It's hard to be so far away from you, to not be able to protect you.”

“I can appreciate that,” Suzie said diplomatically. “But you have to remember that I've been in plenty of dangerous spots before you came along, Paul, and I can handle myself.”

He reached up and lightly stroked her cheek as he gazed into her eyes. “I have no doubt,” he murmured. “Just like Mary has been through very difficult times, and has made it through.”

“Oh you,” Suzie slapped him playfully on the shoulder. “I see what you did there.”

"Do you?" he wiggled his brows. "I thought it was pretty good."

"It was," Suzie sighed. "But I'm still going to investigate."

"Oh, I know you are," Paul said with a short laugh. "I'd be a fool if I thought you weren't. Just be careful. Make sure Jason is helping you."

"I will," she promised him. "Even though I've pulled myself out of a few dangerous situations, Paul, you'll always be my favorite rescuer."

"Aw, that's sweet," he said and slipped his hand into hers. As they started to walk again he stole a glance over at her. "I love you, Suzie."

"I love you, too, Paul," she said and hugged his arm.

***

After Paul dropped Suzie at home he left to prepare for his launch. Suzie still felt uneasy. Paul's words had made sense to her, but she was still boiling with irritation at Wes. She tried to distract herself by thinking about the railing and how it might have come loose. She knew that it had to have been tampered with, or maybe she just really hoped it had been. What she couldn't figure out was who would have wanted Warren dead.

"Suzie, is that you?" Mary called out from the laundry room.

"Yes, it's me," Suzie called back. "Need help?" she asked when she stepped into the laundry room.

"I'm just getting fresh sheets ready for the bed in room five," she explained.

"I don't think anyone will be sleeping in them for a long time," Suzie said with a sigh. "I still can't believe it happened. But everyone in town can, and they think that it was an accident, or possibly negligence."

"We know better," Mary reminded her but she could see the doubt in Mary's eyes.

"I just don't know how to convince others of that," Suzie said still partly trying to convince herself.

"Me neither," Mary agreed as she shook out the sheet she had just pulled out of the dryer. "You and I both know there is no way that railing gave way."

"We had every balcony inspected," Suzie recalled and narrowed her eyes. "Maybe the inspector made a mistake."

"No way," Mary shook her head. "He was very reputable. Besides, we did a walk through with him, and I distinctly remember him leaning on the railings to show us they were strong."

"Yes, that's true," Suzie nodded. "I remember that now. But still, maybe we did cut corners."

"Don't talk like that," Mary said firmly. "There's no way we would have cut corners when it comes to a safety issue."

"You're right," Suzie leaned back against the wall of the laundry room. "Did you hear anything more about the murder from Wes?"

"Actually I did," Mary nodded. Her

expression darkened. “He said he was sorry about the death, and that he would do his best to help us out if he could, but it's not his jurisdiction so he can only investigate so much. Can you believe that?” Mary narrowed her eyes.

“Well, it's not his jurisdiction,” Suzie pointed out. “Not only that, Jason can barely help us because it's being ruled accidental and I think he believes it is.”

“That's not the point is it, Suzie?” Mary snapped. Suzie's eyes widened. It wasn't often that Mary actually got upset.

“I'm sorry,” she said quickly.

Mary sighed and set down the folded sheet. “No, I'm sorry, Suzie. I didn't mean to snap at you. I know you're right. It's just, I expected him to swoop in and take charge I guess. I don't know, maybe you're right, maybe I have been reading too many romances.”

“There's nothing wrong with romance,” Suzie said gently. “All I'm saying is that Wes' hands probably really are tied. Just like Jason's."

"But he didn't even come over to check on me," Mary pointed out. "Of course, I told him not to," she frowned.

Suzie pulled her into a warm hug. "These things are never easy, Mary. But no matter what happens, we'll get through it together."

"I know," Mary said as she hugged her back. "If there's one thing in this world I know I can rely on, Suzie, it's our friendship."

"That's for sure," Suzie said with a laugh. "Now, I think we have earned some wine and chocolate. What do you say?"

"Heavy on the chocolate, light on the wine," Mary requested as they walked into the kitchen.

Chapter Eight

Early the next morning Suzie headed to the library to check on Louis. She made a few stops along the way for party supplies, since Mary was not with her. She was more than a little concerned about how Louis had behaved the day before. She knew that he was likely still taking Warren's death very hard. When she arrived at the library she was surprised to see that there was a police car in the parking lot. When she stepped inside the library she spotted Jason and his partner, Kirk, standing at the front desk with Louis. Louis was red in the face and obviously frustrated.

"Look, I don't know who would have done it," Louis said, clearly aggravated. "I think that you need to be out looking for the criminal who stole my most valuable possession, rather than wasting your time here asking me the same questions over and over again."

"Louis, I'm just trying to get as much

information as possible so that I can solve the crime," Jason said calmly.

"What's going on?" Suzie asked as she walked up to them both.

Jason cast a wary glance in her direction. "Louis had a break-in last night," he explained.

"A break-in?" Louis repeated. "Is that really what you're calling it? The most important thing in my life was ripped out of my home, and you call it a break-in?"

"The book?" Suzie asked and narrowed her eyes.

"Yes," Louis said with exasperation. "First Warren was killed, and now this. I don't think I can take any more. If I don't get that book back, I'm going to lose it. I should have left it here, I never should have taken it home."

"Relax, Louis," Suzie assured him. "Jason is a great police officer and he will take care of this for you."

"I can't, I just can't," Louis said tearfully. He

walked off towards the employee lounge of the library. Suzie stared after him sympathetically.

"So, now I'm a great police officer?" Jason asked, reminding her that he was still there.

"Jason, you know I didn't mean what I said," Suzie said with a sigh. "But surely you can see that there is a case here now. Obviously, whoever killed Warren was also after the book."

"Obviously?" he asked and raised an eyebrow. "Is that an investigative term?"

Suzie narrowed her eyes as she studied Jason. She had never seen him so snippy with her before.

"Are you going to tell me that you don't think that there's a connection between the two crimes?" she asked incredulously.

"I'm not saying that, I'm just saying that the evidence isn't there to support that connection," Jason explained and shook his head. "We can't just make assumptions."

"Assumptions like I must be lying about the renovations I did on the house?" Suzie asked.

"I never said you were lying," Jason pointed out. "Sometimes things are overlooked."

"So, now I'm a liar, and I'm cheap," Suzie said with disbelief. "It's good to know your real opinion of me, Jason."

"Suzie, you know that's not the case," Jason said impatiently.

"Maybe that's the problem," Suzie said with a sigh. "I don't know. What I do know is that this was no accident. Are you going to investigate it as a murder, or not?" she asked.

"I can't," Jason said with a frown. "Not without some kind of evidence. But what I will do is keep an ear out and I will do some investigating and see if any new evidence comes to light. If anything comes up, I will let you know right away."

"Fine," Suzie nodded. She had a million other things she wanted to say, but she didn't think it was appropriate library conversation.

"Suzie," Jason warned her as he met her eyes.

"I want you to stay out of this. No conducting your own investigation. It could come back to hurt you, since the death took place on your property."

Suzie nodded and then walked away from him without saying anything more.

"I mean it, Suzie," Jason called after her. Several people in the library shushed him for raising his voice. Jason shook his head and walked out of the library.

Suzie was more than a little annoyed. She knew that Jason had to do his job, but she felt as if she was the one that was doing it for him. Her cell phone began ringing. She pulled it out to see that it was Mary calling. "Hello?" Suzie asked. She stepped out of the library so that her conversation wouldn't bother anyone.

"Hey Suzie," Mary said. "I just wanted to check on you, and see how Louis is doing."

"Not well," Suzie replied. "Someone broke into his house and stole the book that he was trying to get insured."

"Unbelievable!" Mary said with a shake of her head. "What are the chances of that?"

"Not likely," Suzie replied. "I think that there must be a connection between Warren's death and the stolen book. Of course, Jason doesn't seem to agree," Suzie said and made her best attempt not to roll her eyes.

"Do you think that there is a way we can get some proof that it was connected?" Mary suggested.

"I don't know what proof that would be," Suzie sighed as she walked towards her car. "I can't really blame Jason, there simply is not any evidence. Even the person who stole the book left no evidence behind."

"Well, come home, we'll have lunch and brainstorm," Mary said. "I hate to say it, Suzie, but we may need to focus more on damage control than the murder investigation."

Suzie grimaced as a group of women walking past all began whispering and glaring in her direction. “I think you might be right about that,” she said. Suzie was just about to get into her car when she heard footsteps behind her. She froze, and then slowly began to turn. She found Louis standing just behind her.

“Sorry if I scared you,” he said nervously. His eyes were red-rimmed. Suzie knew how much that book had meant to him.

“It's okay, Louis,” Suzie said gently.

“I heard what Jason said,” Louis explained. “That he didn’t think there was a connection between the death and the robbery.”

“He might be right,” Suzie said in a mild attempt to defend her cousin.

“I get that,” Louis nodded. “But I think there’s a strong possibility that there is a connection between Warren's death and the book being stolen. I was wondering if you would help me?”

“Help you what?” Suzie asked as she met his eyes.

“I need to find out the truth so I want to

investigate this crime," Louis said. "I can't just leave this up to the police. I can't even feel safe in my own home right now."

Suzie knew that she couldn't let it go either. "Louis, you think about all of the people in your life that might have done this. Write a list of their names. Then, we will meet later this afternoon to go over them. Right now I'm going home to try to do some damage control for Dune House, but as soon as you have that list put together, call me and let me know."

"How will I know who to put on the list?" Louis asked as he looked up at her. "I don't have any enemies."

"Start with people that you think would have an interest in the book then," Suzie said. "And add anyone who is shady or has made your skin crawl."

"I can do that," Louis nodded. "Thanks, Suzie."

"Call me when you have your list," Suzie

reminded him before ducking into her car.

Chapter Nine

When Suzie arrived at Dune House, Mary was waiting for her.

"How did it go?" she asked as they shared a quick lunch of salad and half sandwiches.

"Not good," Suzie shook her head. "The worst part is that Jason is getting really testy. He told me to stay out of it entirely."

"He's only trying to protect you," Mary pointed out grimly. "Kids that age think that they know everything."

"I feel like I'm having to prove myself to my cousin, at the same time that I am trying to solve a murder."

"Well, you and Jason really don't know each other very well," Mary reminded her. "You've only been part of his life for a short time, and now you see each other just about every day. It's going to take some time for him to fully trust you."

“I guess you're right,” Suzie sighed. “But I am not going to sit back and let the reputation of this beautiful place that we have restored be tarnished by rumors.”

“What can we do?” Mary asked. “We're at a dead end.”

“Not necessarily,” Suzie said thoughtfully and then took the last bite of her sandwich.

“What are you thinking, Suzie?” Mary asked.

“I'm going to check in with Dr. Rose,” Suzie said as she picked up her purse.

“Didn't Jason say to drop it?” Mary reminded her as she followed Suzie to the door.

“Last time I checked it's not illegal to drop in on a friend,” Suzie called back over her shoulder as she opened the door.

“I think you better think about this, Suzie,” Mary warned her. “I'm sure if you just ask Jason to check...”

“No, I don’t want to bother him,” Suzie said

sternly. "I am going to make sure that we get to the bottom of this."

"Okay, but call me if she found anything, promise?" Mary caught her arm before Suzie could get out the door.

"I promise," Suzie said and paused to smile at Mary. "Don't worry, I won't spend your birthday in jail."

"Good," Mary sighed. "Because last time I had to bail you out it involved going into neighborhoods that weren't exactly safe and friendly."

"Don't worry," Suzie said firmly and tried not to laugh at the memory that Mary stirred up. Then she headed for her car. Mary watched from the door until Suzie pulled out of the parking lot.

Suzie turned on her radio to try to drown out her thoughts. She didn't like to be on the outs with Jason. She knew that he was just trying to do his job. But it hurt that he didn't seem to believe that she had been as careful as she claimed with the updates on the balcony.

When she reached the medical examiner's office, there were no other cars in the parking lot. She stepped out of her car and ducked inside. There was no one at the front desk, but Suzie could hear music coming from the examination room. She knew that Dr. Rose liked to listen to music while she worked. Suzie walked up to the door and knocked lightly.

"Hello? Dr. Rose?" Suzie called out. When there was no answer she pushed the door slightly open. "Summer?" she called again. "Are you in here?"

The music suddenly turned off.

"Suzie?" Dr. Rose poked her head around the corner of the hallway. "Sorry, I didn't hear you out there. Come on back."

Suzie smiled at her. Ever since Dr. Rose and Jason had begun dating, Dr. Rose had been even friendlier to Suzie. She was just hoping that Jason hadn't warned her not to tell her anything about the exam.

“Hi,” Suzie said as cheerfully as she could. “Sorry for interrupting.”

“It's okay,” Dr. Rose said as she snapped off her gloves and tossed them in a disposal bin. “I'm finished.”

“Were you working on Warren Blasser?” Suzie asked nervously.

Dr. Rose settled her gaze on Suzie. “I don't think I should discuss the results with you.”

“Oh, of course not,” Suzie said mildly. “I don't want any details or anything, I was just wondering if you had found any evidence of assault.”

Dr. Rose cleared her throat. “Suzie, I know how difficult it must be for you that this happened at Dune House. But the truth is, there is no evidence of anything other than an accidental fall.”

“Which I would have told you, if you had waited for me to do my job, instead of doing what I asked you not to,” Jason said from just behind

Suzie. Suzie frowned as she hadn't even heard him walk up behind her.

"I'm sorry, Suzie," Dr. Rose said. "I wish that I could tell you something different, but the injuries are consistent with an accidental fall."

"Okay," Suzie said, and closed her eyes. She could feel Jason glaring at her.

"There was no reason to interfere," he said sharply to her. "I told you, if Dr. Rose found anything, you would be the first to know."

Suzie took a deep breath. "I know, Jason, I'm sorry."

"You can't just take advantage of my relationship with Summer," Jason began to say, he was preparing to launch into a full force lecture, which made Suzie quite uncomfortable, since she was old enough to be his mother.

"Jason," Dr. Rose said and laid her hand lightly on his arm. "It's okay. It's not a big deal. She's just worried about Dune House."

"No," Suzie said sharply. "I am not worried

about Dune House, because I already know that this death wasn't an accident. What I'm worried about is a murder going unsolved."

Dr. Rose studied her with some sympathy. "If it's easier for you to believe that he was murdered, that is up to you, Suzie, but there is nothing to indicate that. I know that a tragedy like this happening on your property is overwhelming."

"No," Suzie shook her head. "You're both wrong. Just because there isn't proof, doesn't mean that it didn't happen."

"Suzie, I think you're letting this get out of control," Jason warned her. "What you need to be doing right now is consulting a lawyer and reviewing your insurance."

"Thank you for your time," she said in a clipped voice to Dr. Rose. Without another word to Jason she spun on her heel and walked out of the medical examiner's office. She was nearly to her car when Jason caught up with her.

"Suzie, please don't be upset," he said

urgently. “I didn't mean to be so offensive. To be honest, the results were a surprise to me, too. I really thought maybe you were right, that it was deliberate. I was a little shocked when that didn't turn out to be the case.”

“I still believe it, Jason. If we don't do anything to stop all of this we're going to have an unsolved murder in the town of Garber,” Suzie promised him.

“Suzie, I always have your back,” Jason reminded her and met her eyes. “If there's more to this, I assure you I will uncover it.”

Suzie glanced up at Jason. She wanted to believe him.

“I know,” she said quietly. “I'm sorry that I interfered.”

“Suzie, what about the party?” Jason asked. Those words coursed quickly through Suzie. She knew that she had been distracted and the party was coming up fast.

“It's still on,” she said before she hurried

towards her car. She could feel Jason watching her. She thought he was trying to make sure that she actually got in her car. But when she turned back to look, he was nowhere to be seen. She had a sudden uneasy sensation that maybe it was somebody else that was watching her.

***

Suzie was about to return to Dune House when her cell phone began ringing.

"Suzie, I have the list," Louis said when she answered. "Can you meet me at the library?"

"Sure, I'm two minutes away," Suzie said and started her car. She drove to the library. It looked pretty dead, with only a few cars in the parking lot. As she walked in, Louis walked over to meet her.

"Where's the list?" Suzie asked.

"It's a short list," Louis replied.

"Okay," Suzie frowned. "Who is on it?"

"There's a collector from Florida that is a little obsessive and could possibly border on nuts,"

Louis said grimly. "Tim Barows. Then there is an old high school friend of mine that was always jealous of everything I had. He wanted to be the one to run the school library, instead it was me. That kind of thing."

"Huh," Suzie nodded. So far she hadn't heard anything that made her very suspicious.

"Then, there is Gerald," Louis said with a grimace.

"Gerald?" Suzie asked curiously.

"He's the son of the man who gave me the book. The only reason that I'm even considering him is because the book is rare and valuable, and by all rights should have gone to him," Louis explained.

"Well, that is a pretty good motive," Suzie agreed. "Is it enough of a motive for him to steal and murder someone?"

"I don't think Gerald would do that," Louis said as he shook his head slowly. Then his eyes widened. "Then again, he was always rather snippy with me when I would visit. At the time I thought it was just because his father was sick, and he was stressed. Maybe there was more to it than that," he said. "But I still can't see him as a murderer."

"The book was worth a lot of money, maybe he didn't want to share it with someone who wasn't technically family," Suzie said with a shake of her head. "Once his father was gone, he might have thought he could take it back from you."

"So, you think Gerald broke into my house and stole the book?" Louis asked and frowned. "I don't want to believe it's true, but I can't think of anyone else who would do this."

"What about the other collector that you mentioned?" Suzie asked. "Would he or any other collector you know go to these lengths to get the book?"

"No," Louis shook his head. "A stolen book is worth nothing, all of the other collectors would know that. If a book as rare and valuable as this is reported as stolen there's no way to sell it, or even to show it off, without being arrested."

"Then why would Gerald take it?" Suzie pressed with confusion. "If he couldn't sell it, and he couldn't even show off that he had it?"

"I don't know," Louis admitted. "Maybe just to get back at me. Richard and I had a close relationship. He confided to me once that he had never felt very close to his son. Maybe Gerald was jealous of what we shared, and he just took the book to make sure that I didn't have it."

"I guess that's possible," Suzie nodded. "A personal motive would explain why he wouldn't care about not being able to sell it. However, what in the world could this have to do with Warren's death? What would he get out of killing Warren?"

"Maybe it was just a coincidence," Louis suggested. "Warren could have just fallen..."

"Maybe," Suzie said with sight annoyance. "We did everything we could to ensure the safety of that balcony. I really think that Warren did not just fall. The railing did not just break. I believe it was altered."

"Okay, okay," Louis nodded and backed up slightly. "Let's say that Warren was murdered. That doesn't necessarily mean that it's connected to Gerald and the theft."

"Hmm, good point," Suzie nodded. "Will you excuse me for a moment?" she asked.

"Of course," he nodded and narrowed his eyes. "I can't believe that Gerald would do this," he said to himself.

Suzie was dialing Jason's number as she walked away from Louis. Jason answered on the third ring.

"Suzie, I'm so glad you called," he said. "I know we didn't exactly have a chance to talk everything out and I think that we need to."

"We do," she agreed. "But can we do that later? First, I need you to look into Warren Blasser's past. See if he had any enemies."

"Suzie," Jason sighed. "I told you, I can't do

any investigation when there is no crime."

"I'm not asking you to do any kind of investigation, just to take a glance at the man's past," Suzie pressed impatiently.

"I'll do what I can," Jason replied before hanging up the phone.

When Suzie turned back to Louis she found that he was at his computer.

"What are you doing?" Suzie asked curiously as she walked up to him. She could tell that he was very focused on what he was doing.

"I'm just looking into Gerald's history a little more," he explained. "It seems he has a lot of properties, he may be in more debt than I realized."

"Then his motive would be even stronger," Suzie agreed.

"Maybe," Louis nodded with a frown. "But he wouldn't gain financially because he wouldn't even be able to sell it."

"One good thing is that if it was Gerald that stole the book then there is a good chance he will still have it," Suzie said. "He can't sell it, and it is too valuable to destroy, so he must still be holding onto it."

"I know where he lives," Louis said. His eyes were narrowed as he stared into space. "I can't believe he would do something like this."

"I just hope he's only a thief," Suzie said with a sigh.

"Do you think Jason would check it out for us?" Louis asked hopefully. Suzie frowned as she recalled the way Jason had spoken to her.

"No, I don't," she said. "Without some kind of proof that it was Gerald who stole the book, all he can do is ask Gerald questions. That will tip Gerald off that he is a suspect. If he does have the book, he'll find a way to hide it or get rid of it, before we can get it back."

Louis winced at the very idea. "I can't imagine never seeing that book again," he said. He was heartbroken, Suzie could see that in his eyes. She felt badly for Louis. He could be a little snippy and arrogant, but he was always willing to help when they needed it. He was so surprised when he had an amazing gift given to him, only to have it taken away from him again. But Louis wasn't the only person that she was thinking about. She was thinking about Warren Blasser as well, whose death she was certain was connected with this theft.

"I think we should go ourselves," Suzie said, lowering her voice.

"Go where?" Louis asked.

"To get the book back, to see if Gerald has it," Suzie explained. "You're still friends with the family, right? We could just pop in for a visit, or maybe to tell him about the book being stolen, since it was once his father's. That will give us a chance to look around."

"What a clever idea," Louis said with a smile of approval. "Are you sure that you want to get involved in this though?" he studied her for a moment. "Won't Jason be upset?"

"There's no harm in asking a few questions," Suzie countered. She did her best to make her voice sound confident.

"I can get someone to man the library today," he said. "Should we go this afternoon?"

"Yes, that sounds good," Suzie nodded. "I have an errand to run, then I'll come back to pick you up."

"Okay," he nodded and then looked into her eyes. "Thank you, Suzie, for helping me."

"Thank me after we get your book back," Suzie said. She felt a subtle thrill race through her as she left the library. She loved going on investigations like this. There were times when she really missed her role as an investigative reporter. Sure, many of her jobs had been on the boring side involving politics or celebrities, but the criminal cases were the most thrilling for her. She had left her career to become an interior decorator to give herself a change of pace, and suddenly she had become the owner of a bed and breakfast. But, she still had the blood of an investigator pumping through her veins.

Chapter Ten

As Suzie drove down the main road, her mind focused on the task at hand. She was on her way to speak to Bill Daub, the contractor she had hired to work on the balconies at Dune House. She turned off the main street and drove about ten minutes into the next town.

Bill Daub's office was at the end of a small strip mall. She parked her car and walked up to the door of his office. Through the glass door she could see that he was speaking heatedly with another man in the office. She hesitated for a moment as she wondered if she had walked in on a private meeting. But when Bill began pounding his fist on the desk in front of him, she instinctively pushed the door open. As soon as she stepped inside the two men stopped arguing. Suzie was a little surprised when it was Detective Brown that turned around to face her.

"What are you doing here?" she asked, too

stunned to think about what she was saying.

"Suzie," he said grimly. His dark brown eyes were flashing with anger. He looked back at Bill. "I was here speaking to this gentleman about his poor construction work."

"What?" Suzie asked. She was confused as she looked over at Bill.

"Suzie, I don't understand how this happened," Bill explained. "If you're planning to sue the company however, we shouldn't be speaking about this."

"Sue the company?" Suzie repeated with disbelief. "This is complete nonsense."

"Suzie, watch what you say," Wes warned her. She glared back at him.

"I am perfectly capable of deciding what I want to say and what I don't want to say," she said sternly. "What happened to Warren Blasser was a homicide, and if you can't see that, then I'm starting to question your ability to be a detective."

"Hey," Wes shot back with aggravation in his

voice. “You need to watch how you're talking to me.”

“Do I?” Suzie asked and stepped closer to him. “Are you going to arrest me for having an opinion, Detective Brown?” she demanded.

He stared at her with shock in his eyes. “Suzie, there's no reason for you to be angry at me. I'm here defending Mary, and you. Do you know the consequences you could face if you are found negligent in the death of this man?”

“There is no way she will be found negligent,” Bill interrupted with frustration.

“That's right,” Suzie said grimly. “Because there was nothing wrong with the railing on that balcony.”

“Somehow it broke,” Wes pointed out.

“Someone had to have tampered with it,” Suzie explained. “That's why I'm here, Bill,” she said as she turned to face the man, who was still quite pale. “I want to know your opinion on what might have happened. Don't get me wrong, I am not accusing you. I checked those railings myself, and I had them inspected, they were perfectly sound. But what could someone do to change that?"

Bill looked between her and Wes. It seemed clear that he didn't want to voice an opinion.

"Bill, I'm not going to sue you," Suzie said with a frown. "I'm just trying to figure out what might have actually happened on that balcony. I need your help to do that."

"We tried to make the railings match the buildings history as much as possible, but I can tell you for sure that the railing was sound when it was built," Bill explained. "If you want me to tell you that it could have gotten weak with weather or the elements in such a short period of time, that's not possible. I only use quality wood and it is fully sealed. There is no chance that the wood could have rotted or even been damaged by high winds."

"Then how did it magically break?" Wes

demanded. He shot a brief glance in Suzie's direction, perhaps to see if she was going to attack him for speaking. Suzie only stared at Bill, waiting for an answer.

"Look, I haven't seen the railing in question, and before you ask, I can't see it," he said firmly. "If I go out there to inspect it, it will be like admitting fault. Suzie, I know that you have no interest in suing me, but that can change. You have to understand, I could lose my business, I could lose everything over this."

"And so could I," Suzie pointed out. "So, I do understand. But hypothetically, let's say there was no visible damage to the wood. There were no wood shavings, no cracks, nothing to indicate it was cut in any way. What else would cause it to give way?"

Bill frowned. He stared down at the top of his desk for a few moments. When he looked back up at Suzie he spoke carefully.

"If I were in a situation where I had a railing

fail like that, I would consider counting the screws to ensure that none were missing. Each screw is important to the strength of the railing, even just a few missing can mean the difference between a solid structure and a weak structure."

"Thank you," Suzie said with a sigh of relief. She didn't recall seeing any screws missing, but she also didn't look. "I appreciate your help, Bill. I want you to know, that even though you might not be able to trust my assurance, I will not be suing you or your company. I know that you still have to protect yourself from potential lawsuits by the family of the victim, so I won't ask you anything else about this. However, please know that I am trying my hardest to figure out what actually happened."

"Good," Bill nodded and offered her his hand for a quick shake. "It is a terrible tragedy," he said with a slow shake of his head. "If I thought it was possible that my company was responsible for it, I would have shut down operations already."

"I know that," Suzie nodded. She passed a

quick look over at Wes. “Detective Brown, please stop questioning this man.”

“I was only trying to help,” Wes said fretfully. Suzie turned and walked out of the office. Wes followed after her. “Suzie wait,” he called out and followed her to her car.

“What is it?” she asked testily. She refused to look directly at him. She was still angry with him for upsetting Mary.

“I just want to know what is going on here,” he demanded. “Why are you acting so upset with me?”

“I'm not,” she replied with a bit of a grimace. She didn’t want Mary upset with her for confronting Wes.

“I think you are,” he growled in return. “But if you don’t tell me, then fine. Would you like help looking at the railing? I could come back with you to do that.”

“No, thank you,” Suzie said grimly. “I can handle things on my own. Please leave Bill Daub alone. He is a good man, otherwise I wouldn't have trusted him with the updates on the balconies. This was no accident, and I plan to prove that."

"If there's anything I can do to help, just let me know," he offered.

"Thank you," Suzie said but she had no warmth in her voice as she opened the door. She had no intention of asking him for help, she was still very angry with him. Wes stared after her as she drove off out of the parking lot. She was fuming as she raced back towards Dune House. She wanted to talk to Wes about Mary, but she knew she couldn't because it wasn't what Mary wanted.

***

Suzie had just pulled into the driveway of Dune House when her cell phone rang. When she saw who was calling she grimaced. She had forgotten all about Louis.

"Hi Louis," she said when she answered.

"Suzie, are you coming to pick me up?" Louis asked.

"Oh, Louis I'm so sorry," Suzie said with a shake of her head. "I got distracted with some things at Dune House. I'll be there shortly."

"Why don't you pick me up at home?" Louis suggested. "I have a few things I can get done while I'm waiting."

"Okay, text me your address and I'll be there in thirty minutes," Suzie said quickly.

"Will do," Louis replied before hanging up the phone.

Suzie hurried into the house. She wanted to check the balcony once more. As she walked towards the stairs she called out to see if Mary was home.

"Mary?" she asked. She caught a glimpse of her friend outside on the deck, but she decided to investigate the balcony before talking to her. She wanted a little time to herself. When she walked out onto the balcony she cautiously walked to the broken railing. She searched for the points where it should have been attached to the balcony. Just as the police had found, there was no damage, no indication that the wood had been splintered, or that anything had been used to pry it apart. She swung the railing into its proper position. She lined it up with the edge of the balcony where it should have connected. It fitted snugly into place. Then she crouched down to take a closer look at the way it was supposed to connect.

Although, most of the screws were accounted for, there were at least four that were missing. They were the screws at the base of the structure, the ones that should have provided the most support. If the screws had been removed, and the remainder loosened, maybe the railing would have easily given way. If the police had noticed the missing screws they had likely assumed that they had fallen off when the railing came loose. Suzie guessed it was still a possibility that it happened accidently, but she strongly believed it had been tampered with.

"What a good plan," Suzie muttered to herself. "If he only touched the screws with a screwdriver, never with his fingertips he would have left no trace of his identity, and no evidence of tampering."

She tore herself away from the balcony and walked back down the stairs to the lobby. Mary was there, with her phone in her hand. She looked up at Suzie.

"What did you do?" she asked as Suzie walked towards her.

"What do you mean?" Suzie asked in return. She was puzzled.

"I mean, I just got off the phone with Wes, he said that he had a very interesting encounter with you today," she said and locked eyes with Suzie.

"Well, I didn't say how angry I was with him," Suzie said defensively. "That should count for something."

"Suzie," Mary said with a slight frown. "I know that you're just trying to protect me, but you really have to let me handle things with Wes."

"I'm sorry, I tried not to show him that I was upset with him," Suzie frowned. "I didn't mean to cause a problem."

"I don't think you did," she replied with a smile. "It means a lot to me that you care so much. But I think Wes was a little frightened of you," she giggled.

"He should be," Suzie replied and narrowed her eyes. "He should be very frightened."

"I love you, Suzie," Mary said and gave her a tight hug.

"I love you, too," Suzie said. "I hope that you can figure things out with Wes. But he needs to stop treating you badly."

"I don't know," Mary sighed. "Maybe I was just overreacting. I can be a little sensitive because of how things were with Kent."

"I understand," Suzie nodded. "I'm headed out, do you need anything?"

"Where are you going?" Mary asked. Suzie was about to tell her, but she stopped herself before she could. She didn't want Mary to get in the middle of things. She had enough on her plate with her birthday and Wes' behavior.

"Just to grab a few things at the store," Suzie explained.

"Oh okay," Mary nodded. "No I don't need anything. I'll see you later tonight."

"Absolutely," Suzie replied.

Suzie rushed back to her car. Now that she had her suspicions of how the railing had been sabotaged, she also knew that there would never be evidence to show that was what had happened, unless she could get a full confession out of the murderer. Her assumption of what had happened would not be enough to protect Dune House from a lawsuit. She had nothing to show that could prove that the balcony was tampered with. As she started her car and drove off, Suzie felt a little bad for not being honest with Mary, but it was only for her protection. She didn't want Mary even more stressed out with her birthday coming up.

Suzie drove towards Louis' house. She had never been to it before, but the town of Garber was very easy to drive through. It was essentially a peninsula and had two main roads. When she found the street Louis' house was on she turned and slowed down to watch for the house numbers. The street was quiet with similar medium-sized houses. Suzie pulled up to Louis' house and parked behind his small orange beetle. She climbed out of the car and walked up to the front door. He opened it before she even had the chance to knock.

"I've been waiting for you," he explained. "But I just need to run to the bathroom, come in for a second will you?"

Suzie hesitated for a moment. She liked Louis just fine when he worked in the library, but she had never really gotten to know him very well. She had been in Garber for a short time, so other than Mary and Paul she felt like she really didn't know anyone in town that well, not even her cousin who she had recently met again after decades of no contact.

"Sure," she nodded a little and stepped just inside the door. Louis rushed down the hall, presumably to the bathroom. Suzie thought his house looked exactly as she would expect it to be. His furniture was neat, his carpet clean, the shelves on the walls were filled from end to end with books. She didn't see a television anywhere in the living room, but there was a fireplace. On the mantle of the fireplace was a book. Suzie guessed it was the one he was currently reading. Curious, she stepped closer to check the title. It was a civil war documentary, not something she was terribly interested in. However, something did catch her eye. There were a few photographs on the mantle. One in particular held her attention. It had three people in it. Louis, an older man, and someone who looked very familiar.

"Suzie?" Louis asked from just behind her, causing her to jump. "Are you ready to go?"

“Who is this, Louis?” Suzie asked as she pointed to the photograph.

“Oh, that's Richard,” Louis sighed sadly. “The one who gave me the book.”

“And the man beside him?” she asked.

“That's his son, Gerald,” Louis nodded a little. “He's the one we're going to see today.”

“Are you sure that his name is Gerald?” she asked as she looked from the picture back to Louis.

“Of course I'm sure,” he said. He offered her a puzzled look. “Why do you ask?”

“Because he looks exactly like a man who checked into Dune House the same night that Warren Blasser did,” Suzie said gravely. “He said his name was John.”

“Are you serious?” Louis asked. “Do you think it was Gerald? Do you think he killed Warren?”

“I honestly don't know,” Suzie said with a slow shake of her head. “He checked out the next morning."

"Well, we're going to see him, now," Louis said hesitantly. "What do you think we should do?"

"I'm sure he'll recognize me if I go in there with you," Suzie frowned. "I don't think you should be alone with him, Louis. He could be a killer."

"I'm not afraid of Gerald," Louis almost laughed. "Trust me, he's not intimidating at all."

Suzie frowned. She knew that she had to let Louis make his own choices. She felt like she was getting a little too controlling.

"Just remember, even if he doesn't seem frightening, if he did this, then he is a murderer," she reminded him.

"I really don't think he could kill anyone," Louis shook his head. "But I'll be careful, I promise."

"We'll take my car," Suzie suggested.

“Fine,” Louis agreed and followed her out the door.

Chapter Eleven

Once Suzie and Louis were in the car Suzie felt a little awkward. She and Louis didn't know each other very well, yet she was taking a bit of a road trip with him. She backed down the driveway and started to drive down the street.

"No, it's the other way," Louis insisted.

"Oops," Suzie nodded and turned around to drive down the road in the opposite direction.

"I still can't believe that Gerald would do this," Louis shook his head. "He was always such a sniveling kid. When he was a teenager I didn't think he was ever going to mature."

"I can't believe I never considered him. He checked in before Warren though. Did you let him know that Warren was coming out to value the book?" Suzie asked.

Louis cringed and glanced over at her. "Oh no, I did," he admitted sadly. "I called him, just to let him know that it was going to be inspected. It just seemed right to let him know. He asked me about the valuer and I assured him he was one of the best. Is this my fault?" he asked with a soft gasp.

"No," Suzie said firmly. "The only one at fault here is the murderer who did this. It was not your fault, Louis," Suzie said with sympathy in her voice. "But it also doesn't make sense, does it?" Suzie asked. "Why would Gerald go to all the trouble of murdering Warren when he didn't even have the book?"

"Maybe he didn't know," Louis said quietly. "Maybe he thought that Warren had the book. Then when he didn't find it in his possession, he came looking for it at my house."

"But why?" Suzie asked again. "Do you really think this could all be over simple jealousy?"

Louis sighed and leaned back in the seat. "I'm not terribly close with my family, what there is of it," he explained quietly. "When it comes to a father and son, I don't think there is anything simple about jealousy. Maybe Gerald had more animosity towards me than I ever realized. Perhaps I should have paid closer attention to him."

"Louis, again, you can't blame yourself," Suzie insisted and turned down the street that Gerald's house was on. "I still think it isn't a good idea for you to go in there alone."

"It might not be," Louis admitted. "But I do think that this is partially my fault. Maybe if I had been kinder to Gerald none of this would have happened. I just want the chance to see him face to face, to talk to him about it."

"I'll be right outside," Suzie said and looked at him with concern. "If anything goes wrong, just shout for me."

"And you'll come in blazing?" Louis asked with a laugh. He swept his gaze over Suzie's slender form.

"Don't underestimate me, Louis," Suzie warned. "I've taken down much larger men when needed."

"I feel safer already," Louis said teasingly. Suzie opened her mouth to argue, but she changed her mind at the last moment. She didn't want to get involved in an argument when Louis was about to go into a dangerous situation. "I'll be fine," he promised her before walking up the sidewalk towards the house. Louis paused in front of the front door and took a breath. Then he knocked firmly on the door. He stood there for a few minutes. Then he knocked firmly again. Louis glanced over his shoulder towards Suzie, who was still sitting in the car. Suzie looked around the driveway. There was a car parked in it, but maybe it was an extra car, or maybe Gerald had gone for a walk. Louis knocked one last time and then began walking back towards her. Suzie opened her door and stepped out of the car.

"I guess he isn't home," Louis said with some disappointment.

"Maybe we should take a look through the windows," Suzie suggested.

"Do you think he'd be foolish enough to leave the book laying out in plain sight?" Louis asked skeptically.

"Well, we're here, and he's not, it might be our only chance to sneak a peek," Suzie pointed out. She began walking towards the house. Louis followed after her. Suzie walked up to the front window. There was a curtain drawn closed. She could see light filtering through. She tried to see through the narrow crack in the curtain but she couldn't make anything out.

"You go that way, I'll go this way," she hissed at Louis. Louis nodded and began walking around the opposite side of the house. Suzie reached a window that appeared to look into a study. There were blinds hanging in the window, but they were open. She could clearly see a table with a laptop on it, and two books beside it. Suzie blinked a few times. She wondered if her blood pressure might have gotten a little too high. She felt as if she was seeing double. When she looked through the window again, she saw the identical books in the same position on a wooden desk.

"Louis!" she called out in a loud whisper. Louis had already walked around the side of the back of the house, he was walking towards Suzie.

"I thought you said that the book was one of a kind?" she asked as she looked over at Louis. Louis looked at her with a puzzled expression.

"It is one of a kind," he said firmly. "Why?"

"Because I see two," Suzie replied and pointed at the window. Louis walked quietly over. He peered through the window at the books on the desk.

"Oh no," he moaned and shook his head. "Gerald must have had a copy made."

"So, which one is real?" Suzie asked with confusion.

"I won't know until I can look at them properly," Louis said and shook his head. "I can't believe he did this."

"We should call Jason and let him know what

we found," Suzie said. "Maybe it will be enough for him to get a warrant so he can search the house for evidence of the murder."

"No, don't do that," Louis said with urgency.

"What? Why?" Suzie asked.

"Because, if Gerald is tipped off that we know about the books he might get spooked and hide them. This might be my only chance to get my book back, Suzie," he frowned. "I know it isn't right, but he stole it first."

"What are you saying?" Suzie asked with concern.

"I'm saying I'm going to go in there and steal it back," Louis explained and tried to open the window. He smiled a little when he found that it wasn't locked.

"Louis wait, you can't go in there alone," Suzie said. Then she tilted her head towards the houses nearby. "Besides, someone might see you."

"I didn't really think about that," Louis sighed. "I'm not thinking about anything to be honest. I just want my book back."

"I understand," Suzie said. "We might be able to use it as proof once we get it back," she frowned. "It'll be dark soon, let's wait just a little while. If Gerald doesn't come home, then we'll go in and get the book."

"Good plan," Louis said. "Any chance you have something to eat in the car?" he asked hopefully. "I'm starving."

"I have some granola bars," Suzie nodded. When they returned to the car she handed him a granola bar, and then opened one for herself. As she took a bite of the granola bar a few pieces of it crumbled onto her lap. She brushed them away onto the floor of the car. When she did she recalled the pistachio shells that had been on the balcony. She also remembered that they hadn't found any kind of wrapper from the bag of pistachios. Not in the trash can, not on the balcony, not in the sand below. Her mind was lingering on this, when Louis lightly tapped the dashboard.

"I think it's dark enough now," he said.

The sun had just set and there was still a glow in the sky, but Suzie agreed with him. If they waited much longer, Gerald might arrive home, and then their only chance of recovering the book and proving that he was the thief would be lost.

"Okay, let's do it," Suzie agreed. They quietly crept out of the car. Gerald hadn't come home, so Suzie hoped they would have time to get into the house and back out with the book before he did. They moved stealthily around the side of the house. Suzie and Louis pushed up on the window together until it was high enough for them to crawl through. Suzie held the window up while Louis crawled in, then he did the same for her. Once they were both inside, Suzie turned towards the table where the books had been. Her heart dropped when she saw that the books and the computer were gone. Louis was staring at the same empty table.

"How is that possible?" he asked Suzie in a whisper.

"Maybe we came in the wrong room?" Suzie frowned. She knew that wasn't likely. This was the study she had been looking into earlier. Now it was skewed by darkness, but it was the same room. Suddenly she came to an uneasy realization. Before she could voice it, she heard a noise in the hallway. Then in the darkness, Suzie could see a light flick on underneath the door of the study.

"Louis," she hissed. "Someone is in the hallway."

Louis started moving towards the window they had crawled in, but he knocked over a lamp along the way. The lamp crashed to the floor.

Suzie froze. She was certain that they were about to get caught. She noticed a coat hanging on the hat rack a few feet from her. With nothing to lose, she ducked under the coat hoping that it would shield her. Louis dove down behind the couch.

"Who is in there?" Gerald demanded from the

dark hallway.

Suzie cringed. This man was a potential murderer, at the very least a burglar. She held her breath as she waited to see if he would open the door to the study. As she expected, she heard the click of the knob being turned. She heard the creak of the door slowly swinging open. She could hide and wait for him to find her, or she could try to take him by surprise. She abruptly flung the coat off her and shouted, "We know what you did, Gerald!"

Gerald gasped and jumped backwards. The coat tangled around his feet, causing him to stumble. When he reached for the wall to catch himself he missed completely and fell backwards with a crash. Suzie and Louis started to run past him.

"Wait, wait please," Gerald cried out from the floor. "My back," he moaned.

Suzie slowed to a stop. Louis turned back to look at Gerald.

"See, I told you," he said to Suzie. He sighed and reached down to offer Gerald a hand up. Suzie was not nearly as trusting. She stood back as she watched Louis help Gerald to his feet.

"Louis?" Gerald asked tearfully. "Why would you do this to me?"

"Why would I do this to you?" Louis said in exasperation. "You're the one that broke into my house and stole my book!"

"Are you also responsible for the murder of Warren Blasser?" Suzie asked.

"No!" Gerald said sternly. "All right listen," he took a deep breath and then sighed. "I am guilty of one thing. When my father told me he intended to leave the book to you, Louis, I was jealous, and greedy. I wanted to keep it. So, I spoke to my contacts and I had a forger copy the book. I figured you would never know the difference as I knew you would never try to sell it, so I didn't see how anyone would get hurt," he shook his head. "It was stupid, I know that now."

"Then why did you pretend to be someone else when you stayed at Dune House?" Suzie demanded. "The very same place that Warren Blasser stayed at the same time and where he was killed."

"Please no," Gerald shook his head and looked pleadingly at Louis. "Let me explain," he said quickly. "I didn't even know that man was staying there. When Louis told me that Warren was coming out to value the book, I freaked out. I knew that he would be able to tell that it was a fake. I called Larry, the guy I got to forge a copy. He told me that I better take care of the problem, that he had just been released from jail and he didn't want to go back there. He said all I needed to do was switch the books if I didn't want to end up in jail. So, I stayed at Dune House and planned to break in to Louis' house that night. I was just going to switch the books, so that he would have the real one, and that would be the end of it. But I chickened out when I realized Warren was staying there as well. I called Larry again to tell him that it was too late, he said not to worry, and that he would take care of it. I thought that meant he would steal the book," his eyes filled with tears as he shook his head. "You have to understand, I don't think like a criminal. When I found out that Warren was dead, I was really scared. I knew that it could all come back on me, especially if the book was found to be a fake. I tried to call Larry but he wouldn't answer. So, I broke into Louis' house to swap the books over."

"Likely story," Suzie said as she crossed her arms. "I almost believe you. Except for the fact that you have both books."

"I didn't mean to," Gerald gasped out. "I was going to switch them, but I heard a noise, and I panicked. I had put both books down on a table, and I couldn't tell which was real and which wasn't. My mind was spinning. So, I just grabbed both of them and took off."

"Oh, Gerald," Louis said and ran his fingertips across his forehead. "This is insane."

"But it sounds true," Suzie admitted as she shook her head. "So, you didn't kill Warren?"

"No!" Gerald nearly shouted. "I would never kill anyone! Here," he said and walked over to a painting on the wall. He lifted the painting to reveal a safe. He opened the safe and took out the book.

"How do we know that it's the right one?" Louis asked skeptically.

"Check the stitching," Suzie said. "Warren had it circled on the pictures that you sent him. Maybe he had already figured out it was a fake."

Louis ran his fingertips along the spine of the book and then nodded. "You're right it is different. This is the real copy."

"See?" Gerald said helplessly. "I screwed up, Louis, I'm not going to lie. I was expecting to inherit everything from my father. But I tried to fix things in the end."

"So, that you wouldn't go to jail," Louis accused.

“And with the help of a criminal, a good man ended up dead,” Suzie said.

“I know, I know,” Gerald said and hung his head. “When I saw you two knocking on the door earlier I was afraid you had figured out everything, that's why I pretended that I wasn't home. Are you going to call the police?”

Louis met Suzie's eyes.

“We should,” Suzie said.

“He recently lost his father,” Louis pointed out. “He didn't kill Warren.”

“But he still stole from you, and broke into your house...”

“Just like we just did,” Louis reminded her. “I think we should try to keep Gerald's name out of this as much as possible. It's what Richard would have wanted.”

“All right,” Suzie frowned. “But only if you give us all of the information that you have about this forger you used.”

“All I know is his name and cell phone number,” he said and shook his head.

“What about places you met?” Suzie suggested. “Was there anywhere that you exchanged money or met to talk?”

“Yes,” Gerald nodded. “A dive bar, Smokies, on 5th and Terrace in Parish. We met there a few times,” he nodded. “The bartender seemed to know him fairly well, always got out some nuts for him when we arrived.”

“Okay good,” Suzie nodded. “We can keep your name out of this for now, Gerald, but I suggest you hire yourself a good lawyer.”

“Here's Larry’s number,” Gerald said and jotted down the phone number. “Please, please, believe me. I would never kill anyone.”

“I do believe you,” Louis said and shook his head. “Gerald, I know that your father taught you better than this.”

“I know he did,” Gerald nodded. “I know it. I'm going to try to do better by him.”

As they left Gerald's house it was hard for Suzie to resist calling Jason. She wanted him to know what had happened, and that there was even more reason to believe that Warren had indeed been murdered. But she had made an agreement with Louis about trying to keep Gerald out of it, and she wasn't going to back out on it.

"Let's find this bar," Suzie said. "Do you have any idea how to get there?"

"Yes, it's not too far," Louis said. "But do you really think he'll be there?"

"He thinks he's gotten away with murder, he has no reason to hide out," Suzie frowned.

Chapter Twelve

Suzie and Louis drove towards Smokies. She took the directions that Louis gave her. Within twenty minutes they were outside of Smokies. As Suzie parked, something caught her eye. There was a dusty mustard colored car in the parking lot.

"Louis! That's the car I saw outside Dune House the night that Warren Blasser checked in," Suzie said with excitement in her voice. "It must be Larry's car!"

"I don't think that there could be two cars that ugly," Louis said as he frowned. They stepped inside the bar, which lived up to its name. It was filled with billowing smoke. Suzie scrunched up her nose. She was fairly certain that smoking was banned in most bars now, but that didn't seem to matter to the patrons at Smokies. Suzie walked up to the bar and glanced at the few customers that were seated on bar stools. She spotted one man steadily shelling nuts and popping them into his mouth.

"Larry?" Suzie asked as she locked eyes on him. Larry started to jump up off the bar stool but before he could, Louis was standing on the other side of him.

"Relax Larry, we just want to talk," Louis said with a slight frown.

"I've got nothing to talk about," Larry said with a slow shake of his head.

"Maybe you would like to talk about Warren Blasser?" Suzie suggested. Larry popped another nut into his mouth.

"I have no idea who that is," he shrugged.

"I don't believe you," Suzie said.

"And?" Larry sneered. "I don't have to prove myself to you."

"You will have to prove yourself to the police," Suzie shot back.

"Police?" Larry said with a deep laugh. "I

don't see any police here. Do you?"

Suzie grimaced. She knew that Larry was right. She did not have enough proof to get Jason to arrest this man.

"You're not going to get away with this, Larry," Suzie said firmly.

"I have no idea what you're talking about," Larry scowled. "You're crazy."

"So, you didn't forge a copy of a very rare and expensive book?" Louis asked.

"Oh, fans of my artwork," Larry nodded a little. "Well, I can't say if I did or I didn't, but I can say, you've got nothing on me. If you don't mind, I'm trying to enjoy my beer."

"You listen to me, Larry," Suzie said and leaned towards him.

The bar tender wiped a rag across the bar top in front of her.

"Lady, if you and your boyfriend ain't buying, you need to get out," he said sharply. Suzie sighed and backed away from Larry. The last thing she wanted to do was support a bar that harbored criminals and cigarette smoke and in addition she didn't think she was going to get anywhere with Larry.

Just as Suzie was turning to leave she heard a familiar voice. Her gaze shifted to a booth. There, to her surprise sat Detective Brown. Her voice caught in her throat. She was tempted to alert him that she had seen him, to question him, or to demand that he help with the investigation, but she remembered what Mary had said. She didn't have a right to interfere. Detective Brown leaned forward to talk to the person in a trench coat across from him. Suzie couldn't hear what he was saying.

"Out, now," the bartender said again and pointed towards the door.

"We better go, Suzie," Louis said gravely.

"Fine," Suzie nodded. As they left the bar, she wrote down the license plate number from the back of Larry's car. She was silent as she drove Louis back to his house.

"Do you want to come in for a minute?" Louis offered. "We could talk about what we've found out so far."

Suzie nodded a little. She wasn't ready to face Mary yet after what she had seen.

Once she was settled in Louis' living room he handed her a bottle of water.

"So, what did you think of Larry?" he asked.

Suzie sighed. "I think he must have murdered Warren, but how are we going to prove it?" she shook her head. "I just feel like we're getting nowhere with this," Suzie admitted.

Louis had opened his laptop and was tapping lightly on his keyboard.

"We did get the book back," he pointed out.

"I know," Suzie admitted. "Which is a good thing. But can we really let Warren be buried with people believing that his death was an accident?"

"Unfortunately, we don't have any proof of Larry's involvement, if it was even Larry," Louis pointed out. "Just because you saw a car similar to his at Dune House, that doesn't make him a murderer. We still have no idea how he did it, or why he would have done it."

"Well, we know that he's a forger, that he may have been trying to protect himself from getting caught," Suzie pointed out.

"But he didn't need to go to the extreme of killing Warren," Louis stated. "Besides that, he didn't have the book. It was at my house. So, even if he killed Warren that wouldn't solve the problem of him not getting caught. Some other valuer would have detected the fraud."

"You may be right about that," Suzie said softly. "There doesn't seem to be a motive for Larry to kill Warren."

"So, there you go," Louis shrugged.

"No," Suzie shook her head. "That's not what I meant. What I meant was there must have been a reason. Maybe that's what we're missing. Maybe there was some kind of personal connection between Warren and Larry. Something that would make Larry more prone to commit murder than just the fact that there was a fraudulent book."

"Hmm, but what?" Louis shook his head. "I can't see their paths crossing for any reason."

"Wait," Suzie snapped her fingers. "Larry had just gotten out of jail right?"

"Yes," Louis nodded. "I believe that is what Gerald mentioned."

"What was he in jail for?" Suzie asked. "Can you look it up on the computer and find out?"

"Sure," Louis nodded. He spent a few minutes typing things into the computer. Suzie's mind was slowly churning. She was beginning to formulate a theory.

"Looks like he did five years for fraud," Louis said quietly. "It doesn't say what type of fraud."

"Okay," Suzie said. "That makes sense, as we

know that he is a forger. But we also know that he's very good. So, how did he get caught? Does it list the witnesses who testified against him?"

Louis typed some more information into the computer. Suzie leaned forward so that she could see the results as well when they came up. "Anything?" she asked.

"Absolutely," Louis said. "One of the star witnesses was Warren Blasser. He proved that the antique that Larry had been trying to pass off as a priceless object was in fact a very well designed copy."

"There you go," Suzie said and smiled as she sat back in her chair. "A personal connection. So, like Gerald said, he hired him to forge a copy of the book that his father intended to pass down to you. Once that was done he switched the books, which his father was not aware of in his ill state. So, I think that the book that you received was always the copy," Suzie explained.

"That makes sense," Louis grimaced.

"Though, I hate to admit that I didn't realize it wasn't the original."

"You would have no reason to suspect it, Louis," Suzie pointed out. "You trusted Richard. You knew he would never give you a copy. It was really the perfect crime, until you told Gerald that Warren Blasser was coming to town to value the book. Then he called Larry in a panic. Larry gave him the plan to steal the copy and replace it with the genuine book. Then Larry found out it was Warren Blasser that was coming to town. He knew that Gerald might not follow through. He knew that Warren would see through his work, as he had in the past, and send him back to prison. So, rather than risk it, and perhaps to get a little revenge, he attacked Warren before he could ever even see the book."

"Wow," Louis shook his head. "If that's all true, then how did he kill Warren?"

"That is still a mystery," Suzie admitted. "I don't know how he could have done it. Maybe Gerald helped him?"

“I still don't think he was involved,” Louis said. “He's a weasel, there's no question about that, but a murderer?”

“You may be right,” Suzie said. “I think the key here is Larry. He obviously had the most to lose if Warren had lived. Maybe he didn't care if another valuer looked at the book, as long as it wasn't Warren.”

“But we still have no proof,” Louis pointed out. “We can't prove that it was Larry's car at Dune House. We can't prove that he was ever even there. We can't even prove that he was involved in the forgery unless we can get Gerald to admit to the police that he hired him.”

“Which I doubt he will do,” Suzie agreed. “I think the only thing that we can do is go to Larry's house. Maybe there will be proof there. Or maybe if we talk to him, he will slip up about what he has done.”

“Maybe, but I still don't think it's a good idea to confront him,” Louis said grimly. “We're talking about a hardened criminal here, Suzie, a killer."

"I know that," Suzie said in return. "But if we don't find something to implicate him, he's going to get away with it. That's not something I can stand happening. If you don't want to be involved, Louis, I understand."

"There is no way you're going anywhere without me," Louis said sternly. "I may not be the bravest man in the world, I may not be the most muscular, but I'm not about to run away from a dangerous situation. I just think we should go to the police with what we have, just so they know what we're up to."

"We can't," Suzie said gravely. "If Jason finds out that I still have my nose in all of this, he is not going to be happy. Trust me."

"All right," Louis nodded. "Then we'll go on our own."

"Can you find his address?" Suzie asked.

"I already have it," Louis said as he hit the

button on his keyboard to print the document on his screen.

"Great," Suzie nodded. "Then we should go as soon as possible, before he has the chance to skip town."

"I'm ready when you're ready," Louis said and snatched the paper out of the printer.

"In the morning," Suzie said. "I'm exhausted, you're exhausted, and I feel better about doing this in daylight."

"Okay," Louis agreed. "Are you okay to get home?"

"Yes," Suzie nodded. "Louis, will you pick me up at Dune House at seven tomorrow morning, that way Mary can have the car if she needs it. We'll head straight out to Larry's house."

"You got it," Louis nodded.

***

On her drive home Suzie had a hard time staying focused on the road. She glanced in her rearview mirror and realized all of the party decorations she had bought were still in the backseat. She sighed and parked in the parking lot of Dune House. Everything looked dark, so she assumed that Mary was sleeping. She grabbed the bags from the back seat and headed inside. She was walking down the hallway when Mary flicked the hall light on.

"Where have you been, young lady?" she asked.

"Shopping," Suzie said and hid the bags behind her back.

"Oh, I see," Mary said with a sly smile. "Keeping secrets?"

"Only good ones," Suzie replied. "Now off to bed with you, before you ruin the surprise."

"All right, just remember, I'm not that fond of surprises," Mary warned her. Suzie tried not to grimace. She wondered for a moment if the party was a bad idea altogether. Once Mary had headed back to her room, Suzie hurried into her room and tucked the bags into her closet. Then she collapsed onto her bed. All of the running around really had left her exhausted. But as she tried to sleep her mind kept filling with Larry's laughter. They might not have any proof, but she was sure that he was the killer. When she finally fell asleep she dreamed about pistachios.

Chapter Thirteen

First thing in the morning Suzie slipped out of Dune House. She didn't wait to see if Mary was awake. Mary might ask too many questions, and Suzie might not be able to lie well enough to her. She didn't want to risk Mary finding out that she intended to confront a murder suspect, or risk the possibility that Mary would follow after her. Louis was waiting in the driveway.

"Suzie?" she heard Mary call out as she reached his car. She was standing on the front porch still in her nightgown.

"I'm just going into town for a little bit with Louis," Suzie waved to Mary.

"Okay," Mary called back. She narrowed her eyes and then hurried back into Dune House. Suzie hoped that she wasn't upset with her. When she got in the car, Louis had already stopped for coffee and muffins.

"Thank you so much," she said as he handed

her a coffee. He settled into the passenger seat.

"Hey, we can't confront a killer on an empty stomach," Louis said grimly. "Hopefully we can get him to confess something incriminating," he added quietly.

"Hopefully," Suzie nodded as she had a sip of her coffee.

"If only we knew something that might connect him to the crime."

"I think I might," Suzie replied in a murmur.

"What is it?" Louis asked eagerly.

"I'll let you know when I find out if I'm right."

As they drove to Larry's house they were both fairly silent aside from slurping coffee and munching on the muffins. Suzie knew that Louis wasn't used to this kind of activity, in truth she wasn't used to it either, not any more. She had become much more used to renovating and decorating than investigating.

They parked a short distance from the

driveway that led up to Larry's house. The driveway was empty when they arrived.

"Now what?" Louis asked.

"Now, we wait," Suzie replied with determination. "Let's get closer," she suggested.

The two left the car behind and walked to the end of the driveway. It was a corner lot that backed up to the woods, so there was a good amount of brush surrounding the driveway. Suzie and Louis crouched down behind it. Not a minute later they heard the rumbling of an engine.

"Is that him?" Louis asked and tried to stick his head out.

"He's pulling in now," Suzie said and tugged Louis back into the bushes beside the entrance of the driveway.

"What are we going to do?" Louis asked with fear rising quickly in his voice. "He'll see us!"

"Shh," Suzie insisted. "He won't see us if you quiet down and stay down," she whispered. Louis tightened his lips and lowered his head. The car rumbled past them and up towards the house. The engine turned off. Suzie heard the squeak of the car door as it slowly opened. She closed her eyes for a moment and wondered if it was worth the calculated risk that she was about to take. She could hear the car door beginning to close once more. She knew that once Larry made it into the house, he would have the upper hand. She had to make her move before it was too late.

"Stay here," she hissed at Louis.

"What are you talking about?" he demanded. Without answering she stepped out from behind the bushes.

Larry was just about to slam the door shut when Suzie called out to him. "Larry? Do you have a moment?"

He froze, the door still slightly open. Then he looked slowly over his shoulder.

"What are you doing here?" he asked gruffly.

"I'm sorry, I know this must seem strange to you. When we were at the bar the other day, I noticed that you were enjoying those pistachios so much. I was wondering if you knew where to find some, not just the run of the mill pistachios, but the best pistachios," she said with a soft laugh.

"What are you talking about?" Larry demanded with irritation. "You stalked me, you followed me all of the way to my house, over pistachios?" he glared fiercely at her. "You need to get off my property before I call the police!"

"Would you, Larry?" she asked as she moved between him and the house. "Because I am here about the pistachios. I think the police would be very interested in the pistachios as well."

"Have you lost your mind?" he asked sharply. "Why would the police be interested in pistachios?"

"Perhaps they would be interested in the pistachio shells that were found on the balcony that Warren Blasser stood on just before he died," Suzie suggested. All of a sudden Larry's expression grew as hard as rock.

“What did you just say to me?” he asked in a wicked voice.

“You heard me,” Suzie replied daringly. “Is that what you used to coax him out of his room?” she pressed. “Did you throw your pistachio shells up against the window of his room until he stepped out onto the balcony?”

“I have no idea what you’re talking about,” he shook his head. “You are truly mental.”

“I don't think so,” Suzie said grimly. “I also think when the police test the DNA on those pistachio shells, they're not going to find Warren's. They're going to find yours.”

“Why would they test them?” Larry laughed. “It was an accident. A terrible tragedy that occurred because of your negligence. Isn't that what everyone believes?”

“You forget one very important factor in all of this, Larry. My cousin, Jason, is on the Garber police force. All I have to do is ask him to test those pistachios and he will make it happen,”

Suzie locked eyes with Larry to show him that she was not frightened by him.

"Oh, the Garber police?" Larry asked with mock fear in his voice. "How terrifying," he rolled his eyes. "You need to move on before you get yourself hurt."

"I'm not the one who is going to be hurt," Suzie said as she narrowed her eyes. "You murdered a man on my property, and you have to pay for that."

"I didn't do it, and you can't prove I did," Larry nearly shouted back. "You don't have any pistachio shells with my DNA. I'm not stupid. I'm an artist," he growled.

"An artist that has gone to prison for his crimes," Suzie challenged. "That's where you're going back to."

"I will never go to prison again," Larry abruptly roared. His dominant demeanor suddenly became violent as he jerked the door of his car open. Suzie heard the squeak of the door and saw Larry's hand reach into the vehicle for something. She was too startled to do anything to defend herself. She could only watch as he moved swiftly. When he stood back up again he had something in his hand. Suzie was sure it was a weapon. “You should have walked away when I gave you the chance,” he shouted. “Now, you're going to have to be another unexplained fatality.”

Suzie started to take a step back. She heard a twig snap, and expected that Louis had come out from behind the bushes in an attempt to protect her. But before she could create distance between herself and Larry he had his arm around her waist. He jerked her body back hard against his and pinned her there. Suzie could barely breathe as his arm across her stomach was so tight. Then she felt a cold, hard object pressed against the side of her neck.

“Don't take another step,” he growled. Suzie saw Louis standing a few feet away from them, his eyes filled with fear.

“Suzie, don't move,” Louis said as he froze

where he stood. Suzie's heart began pounding. She didn't know exactly what was pressing against her neck but she could feel a point and knew that it had to be made out of metal. Her stomach churned as she wondered if these would be the last moments of her life.

"Get down," Larry commanded Louis.

Louis slowly sank to his knees in the dirt driveway, his eyes locked to Suzie. "Larry, you don't have to do this," Louis said. "This was all a misunderstanding. Obviously you had nothing to do with Warren Blasser's death. Nobody is going to send you back to prison."

Suzie cringed as Larry laughed loudly beside her ear. "Oh yes, we'll all just shake hands and become the best of friends, right?" he shook his head. "Wrong."

Suzie closed her eyes for a moment. She was trying to keep herself calm and her mind clear. She knew that losing focus at that moment would only cause her to make a big mistake.

"Larry, people know we're here," she lied quietly. No one had any idea they were there. She hadn't even told Paul what she was up to. Jason wouldn't have any idea that she and Louis had decided to take matters into their own hands. They were alone with little hope of escape. "If you do this, you won't be going to prison for forgery, you'll be going to prison for murder. You were right, we don't have any proof that you killed Warren. But how do you think you're going to hide something like this?"

"You won't have to worry about that," Larry replied with cruel amusement. "You'll be dead."

He jerked her body hard to the right and began pulling her towards the door of the small house. "You too," he said to Louis. "One wrong move and she's a goner."

Louis looked helpless as he watched Larry drag Suzie. Reluctantly, he stood up and followed after them. Suzie knew that Louis was walking to his own demise. He was only cooperating in an attempt to protect her. He could have fled at any moment. She felt such gratitude towards him. She never would have expected that he would try so hard to protect her.

As Larry walked towards the door to the house, Suzie thought of the birthday party she would be missing. She wondered if Mary would be able to run Dune House on her own, or would she give it up to pursue other things? As Larry started to pull her into the house, she thought about Paul. He had pleaded with her to be cautious, and she hadn't listened. She knew that would be no comfort to him. He had been living a solitary life when she first met him. He had reached out of his comfort zone to be with her, she doubted that he would ever do that again. She hated to think of him living the rest of his life alone.

“Larry, please,” she whispered. “I've done nothing to you. I've never hurt you, just let us go.”

“Not a chance,” he barked in her ear. He seemed to be struggling with the door handle. Suzie met eyes with Louis. She held his gaze. When she knew he was paying attention to her and not Larry, she mouthed a word to him.

"Run!"

Louis shook his head slightly. Suzie mouthed it again. She knew that the moment they were all inside the house there would be no chance of either of them surviving. She didn't want Louis to sacrifice himself for her. Louis hesitated again. She closed her eyes for a moment. She felt Larry finally get the door open. She opened her eyes and looked into his eyes.

"Go," she hissed. "Please!"

Louis grimaced, and then abruptly darted towards the edge of the yard.

"Get back here!" Larry shouted. "She's dead now, she's dead!" he said and Suzie felt the tip of whatever weapon he was using digging into the skin of her neck. She felt tears in her eyes. She had hoped that maybe Larry would be so startled by Louis' escape that he would loosen his grip on her, but he didn't. He was shouting and cursing at Louis, but he was still holding Suzie tightly. Suzie knew in the next second they would be in the house. There was no way Louis would be able to get help in time.

"Let her go," a voice growled from just behind both of them. Suddenly, Suzie realized why Larry was having so much trouble getting into the house. Someone inside the house was holding the door shut.

"Who are you?" Larry growled and tugged Suzie back away from the door.

"It doesn't matter who I am," the person replied. "All that matters is that I am the one with the gun."

Suzie gasped at the word. She also recognized the voice. Her eyes filled with tears. She tilted her head to the side so that she could see Mary standing in the doorway. Not only was she glaring at Larry, she was pointing what appeared to be a very real gun directly at him.

"Like you even know how to use it," Larry chuckled. "Just put the gun down, or this screwdriver goes into her pretty little neck," Larry threatened. Mary raised an eyebrow. Then she released the safety on the gun. Suzie felt Larry shudder at the subtle click of the safety being released.

"All right, all right," he mumbled and hesitantly lowered the screwdriver. Suzie felt a brief sense of relief. Then Larry roared and abruptly shoved Suzie directly at Mary, who was still pointing the gun at Larry. Suzie stumbled and fell into Mary's arms. Mary managed to lower the gun before the collision.

Suzie was so startled by being shoved it took her a moment to gain her composure. Suzie glanced around for Larry but it seemed as if he was long gone. "I guess he got away," she sighed and shook her head. "Mary, I don't know what I would have done if you hadn't been here, you saved my life!"

She turned to see a police car screaming into the driveway of the house. Jason nearly tripped as he jumped out of the car before it had come to a complete stop. He had his weapon drawn as he ran towards the two women.

"Are you okay?" he shouted as he skidded to a stop a few feet from them. His partner, Kirk, was running right behind him.

"We're okay," Suzie said. "But Larry took off into the woods," she pointed into the woods. Jason lifted his eyes from where Suzie was pointing to Mary, who was still nervously holding the gun in her hand. Jason cautiously moved closer to her.

"Give me that gun, Mary," he said as calmly as he could. Suzie could hear the tension in his voice.

"It's not loaded," Mary said as she offered him the gun carefully. Suzie sighed with relief at the realization that it wasn't loaded. Jason held the gun and then he turned to Kirk.

"Go after him," he said tilting his head towards the woods. Kirk's eyes lingered on the gun for a moment, but he slowly nodded. He took off at a fast run into the woods. Suzie continued to hold tightly to Mary.

"Is this your gun, Mary?" Jason asked as he studied her intently.

Mary shifted uncomfortably from one foot to the other. "Not exactly," she replied hesitantly.

"Mary?" Suzie asked with surprise. "Where did you get it from?"

"I'd rather not say," Mary replied with a grimace.

Jason narrowed his eyes. He opened the chamber to ensure it wasn't loaded then he handed the gun back to Mary.

"Jason, I..." Mary started to say.

"Not another word," he warned her sharply. "I don't want to know whose weapon it is. As far as I'm concerned there was never a weapon here."

Mary looked down shamefully and tucked the gun into her purse that hung at her side.

"What about Kirk?" Suzie asked nervously.

"I'll take care of Kirk," Jason assured her. Just

then Kirk radioed Jason to let him know that he had found Larry in the woods. "Is the suspect injured?" he asked.

"No," Kirk's voice came back over the radio. He paused a moment before adding. "Says the ladies have a gun, but I didn't see one."

Jason nodded and smiled a little. "Me neither," he replied.

"The two of you, just don't mention the gun," Jason warned them.

Mary nodded soundlessly. Suzie smiled faintly with appreciation. She knew that Jason was trying to protect them from getting into trouble for being in possession of a weapon that they didn't own. As Jason jogged off into the woods to assist Kirk with Larry, Suzie looked over at her friend.

"It's over now, Mary," she said soothingly.

"I was so scared," Mary sighed.

"I know, so was I," Suzie admitted. "How did you get in the house? How did you even know I was here? More importantly, whose gun is that?" Suzie demanded.

"I think I need to sit down," Mary said as she sank down onto the first step of the small porch of the house.

"Okay," Suzie said softly. "Louis must have called Jason when he ran. But I still don't understand, how did you know we were here?"

Mary shook her head. "I know you too well, Suzie."

"What does that mean?" Suzie asked with confusion.

"It means I knew that you were up to something. I could tell that you were trying to keep me out of it. Which meant that it had to be pretty dangerous. So, when you left with Louis, I followed you. I parked a few houses down and was walking through the backyards so you wouldn't see me. That's when I saw you with Larry. I was behind the house so I tried his back door, and it was open. I walked through the house, and that's when I saw him holding that screwdriver at your neck. I knew that if he got you inside he would hurt you, so I was holding the door shut. When I saw Louis run, I knew that I had to act fast, because Larry was going to panic."

"I told Louis to run," Suzie said gently. "He tried to protect me."

"I know you did," Mary sighed. "Always trying to save others."

"Not this time," Suzie pointed out. "This time you saved me. But I still don't understand whose gun this is?" she asked.

Mary grimaced, "Wes questioned Gerald and found out about Larry, he told me what he had found out about Larry's past and that he suspected there was a connection between Larry and Warren, which led him to believe that Larry really was involved with Warren's death. I knew that it was going to be dangerous, and I knew that you and Louis were going to get in the middle of it. I also knew where Wes kept his extra weapon..."

"This is Wes' gun?" Suzie asked with a gasp. "Does he know you have it?"

"No, absolutely not, he would be furious if he knew. I made sure it wasn't loaded when I got it. I didn't want to hurt anyone I just wanted to protect you," Mary shook her head. "I'm very lucky that Jason didn't take it. Then Wes would be in trouble, too."

"You took a lot of risks, Mary," Suzie admonished. "You could have been hurt or killed!"

"This from the woman who was being held hostage by a murderer?" Mary demanded as she looked into her friend's eyes. "I know that you think I've lived a sheltered life as a wife and mother, Suzie, while you've been out doing adventurous things. But when it comes to you, there is no way I am going to hesitate to do what I have to do to protect you."

Suzie smiled warmly at her words. "I

appreciate that, Mary," she said as she hugged Mary again. "You're right. I didn't want you to get in the middle of all of this. But it's not because I think you're sheltered. It's your birthday, I just wanted it to be a special time for you."

"Well, I held a gun," Mary laughed a little.

"Not a word," Jason warned as he and Kirk emerged from the woods with Larry handcuffed between them. Kirk swept his gaze over the two women. His expression was stoney. Suzie still wasn't sure that he could be trusted, but he didn't seem to be asking about the weapon, and he was the one that said he hadn't seen a gun.

"I guess you'll be going back to prison after all, Larry," Suzie said smugly. "For a much longer time, this time."

Larry scowled at her. Kirk led him to the police car and guided him into the back seat. Louis appeared from the bushes beside the driveway. Only then did Suzie realize he had never really left. He had only hidden.

"Is everyone okay?" he asked as he walked up to Suzie and Mary.

"We will be," Suzie promised him. "Thanks to you calling the police," she added.

"I didn't know what else to do," Louis admitted.

"You did exactly the right thing, Louis," Mary said.

"Jason, we better get him down to the station," Kirk said as he rapped lightly on the roof of the police car. Jason glanced over at him and nodded. When he looked back at Suzie and Mary he frowned.

"I'm going to need statements from all of you," he said grimly. "Do you want me to get another car to bring you down to the station?"

"No, I'm okay to drive," Suzie said. "Jason, Larry is the one who killed Warren Blasser. I think he did it by throwing pistachio shells at his window until he came out onto the balcony. He must have removed the screws from the balcony earlier in the day," she pointed to the screwdriver that was laying on the ground nearby. "I imagine that is what he used. If you search his car you might even find the screws."

"I don't think you need to worry about it," Jason said. "I'm sure he'll confess in exchange for a shorter sentence. But I will have his house, car, and property searched for any further evidence," he started to turn away. Then slowly he turned back to face her. "Suzie, I'm sorry that I didn't believe you straight away. I should have looked into everything more deeply from the start."

"It's okay, Jason," Suzie said. "You were just doing your job. There was nothing to indicate that anything sinister was going on in the beginning."

Jason nodded and then headed off to the police car. Louis sat down on the step beside the two women.

"I think I like being a librarian much better than being a detective," he said grimly. "My heart is still racing."

"Don't worry, soon you'll be back in the nice, safe, quiet library," Mary said with a slight laugh.

"I can't wait," Louis admitted.

"At least you got your book back," Suzie pointed out.

"And as least we cleared Gerald's name as a murderer," Mary stated.

"Yes, Richard would be happy about that," Louis said wistfully. "Gerald might not have been honest, but he was not a murderer."

"We better get going," Suzie said. "Jason will be expecting us. Mary, I think you better call Wes and tell him the truth about his weapon."

"He's going to be so angry," Mary cringed.

"Maybe," Suzie agreed. "But if he has to report one of his weapons missing he's going to be in a lot more trouble with his boss. Better to tell him the truth, just in case anything comes up later."

"I guess," Mary nodded.

"Let's get you home," Suzie said and hugged

her friend. “Tomorrow is your birthday.”

“It is, isn't it?” Mary asked with a vague smile.

“I'm glad to hear that you and Wes are talking,” Suzie said hesitantly. She still wasn't sure if she should tell Mary what she had seen in the bar.

“Me, too,” Mary admitted with a girlish smile. It was that smile that made Suzie keep her mouth shut.

Chapter Fourteen

Suzie and Mary spent the rest of the afternoon fielding interviews by Jason and Kirk, as well as sharing quite a bit of wine. Suzie was fairly sure that there wasn't enough wine in the world to take away the memory of that screwdriver pushed against the side of her neck. When she finally crawled into bed, Suzie felt as if she could sleep for a century. She was finally able to rest, now that she knew Warren's killer was behind bars, and that it wasn't a faulty railing that had killed him. She could only hope that would be enough to save the reputation of Dune House. She fell asleep with plans for regaining the community's trust floating through her mind.

It seemed like a cruel joke when Suzie's alarm began buzzing. She slapped the button to quiet it down. Then she yawned as she stretched out in her bed. She was awake, but did not really want to get up. After the incident the day before, she was savoring the ability to just relax. Then slowly reality began to creep into her sleepy mind. Not only was there no time to relax as party preparations had to be made, Benjamin and Catherine would be arriving in just a few hours.

Suzie suddenly jumped up out of bed. She rushed around her room getting dressed and searching for the lists she had made of party information. One list was for supplies. Another list was for guests. The last list was for the errands she would have to run in order to get everything she needed that day. Just about everything depended on Mary being out of the house. Originally, Suzie had intended to let Wes handle that for her, but since they weren't exactly on speaking terms, she wasn't sure if that was going to happen. She felt a little worried as she padded out into the kitchen. She hoped that Mary might be sleeping in. The scent of fresh coffee indicated that she was not.

“Mary?” Suzie called out. She didn't see her in the kitchen or the dining room. Suzie frowned and then helped herself to a cup of coffee. She thought perhaps Mary had gone for an early morning walk along the beach. She walked over to the side door off the dining room that led onto the beach.

When Suzie stepped out onto the porch, she noticed Mary's robe tossed on the back of one of the lounge chairs. She thought it was a little odd as Mary usually dressed before she went out onto the porch. There was also a cup of coffee, half full on the table in front of the chair. Beside it was a newspaper. Suzie noticed that it was turned to an article about Larry and his involvement in Warren Blasser's death. To Suzie's relief the article did not mention the location of the crime. She was sure that Paul had something to do with that as he knew everyone worth knowing in the town, and he had likely called in a few favors to protect Dune House. Suzie was pleased to see that Warren would be getting his justice, even though it still saddened her to think of him.

Suzie's mind was distracted by the fact that Mary was missing. She couldn't imagine her friend walking along the beach in her pajamas, birthday or not, Mary was much more modest than that. Suzie began walking around the wraparound porch in search of her friend.

"Mary?" she called out. She was beginning to grow concerned.

"I'm over here, Suzie," Mary called back. She was on the rear porch. She had a bunch of flowers in her hands.

"Happy birthday!" Suzie said and gave Mary a quick hug. "What are those?" she asked as she looked at the flowers.

"A gift from Wes," Mary said sadly. "He must have pre-ordered them. He certainly wouldn't want me to have them now."

"What do you mean?" Suzie asked with concern.

"They were delivered early this morning while I was having my coffee. I knew you'd be up soon, I didn't want you to see me upset," she admitted.

"Mary, you don't need to hide your feelings

from me," Suzie said and shook her head. "But, why do you think Wes wouldn't want you to have your flowers if he ordered them for you?"

"Well, because when I returned his gun to him last night, he was quite upset," Mary admitted. "He was furious really. He told me that I never should have taken it in the first place, that it was a very dangerous thing I did, and that he couldn't trust me."

"Oh, Mary I'm sorry," Suzie said and frowned. "I'll talk to him. I'll explain to him how you saved my life."

"No," Mary shook her head. "I don't think there's really a point. He was right. I never should have taken it. He said if I had just told him the trouble I was in he would have been more than happy to help me. He lectured me about going there alone," she sighed and looked out over the water. "You know, I thought I was ready for romance again, Suzie. But, I rather like not having anyone around to lecture me, or have an opinion on my life."

“Hmm,” Suzie narrowed her eyes playfully. “Well, you do still have me,” she reminded her. “I plan to lecture you and have an opinion on your life for a very long time to come.”

“Very funny,” Mary cracked a smile. “But seriously. All of this questioning and mysterious behavior, it has left me exhausted. Is love really worth all of this work?” she shook her head as she looked back down at the flowers. “I guess there's really no reason to even think about it, considering that he wants nothing to do with me now.”

“Did he tell you that?” Suzie asked.

“Not in so many words,” Mary admitted. “But I knew that he meant it.”

“I'm sorry, sweetie,” Suzie said and hugged her. She was absolutely livid inside. She couldn't imagine a man who could be so cruel as to break a woman's heart right before her birthday. Sure he did have a reason to be angry since she did steal his weapon, but that didn't mean that he had to be so hurtful about it. “Maybe he will cool off and come to his senses.”

“To be honest, I'm not so sure that I want him to,” Mary admitted. “He was obviously focused on other things all week. I don't think the message could be much clearer. He is not interested in being part of my life.”

“Try not to think about it too much,” Suzie said. “It's your birthday today, remember?”

“Yes,” Mary smiled. “We should go out together and do something, Suzie. I don't want to spend the whole day thinking about Wes. Would you like to go to the movies or something?” she asked hopefully.

Suzie realized she was in a very difficult position. She had a ton of preparations to complete, including picking up Benjamin and Catherine from the airport. She had no idea how she could do any of it if she was spending the day with Mary. But she knew it would hurt her friend if she turned her down now.

"Why don't we go to lunch and then make plans from there?" Suzie suggested.

"Sounds good," Mary said. She frowned for a moment and then spoke again, "I tried calling both Benjamin and Catherine this morning. I just wanted to hear their voices so I could cheer up. Neither of them answered. I know they're busy, and I really don't expect them to remember that it is my birthday, I just so wanted to hear them."

"They might still be sleeping," Suzie pointed out and tried to swallow back her guilt. "You know how college kids are."

"You're right," Mary shook her head. "I guess I'm just in a funk. I hope I can get out of it soon."

"I'll make sure that you do," Suzie assured her. "I'm going to make us some pancakes," she said decisively.

"That sounds delicious," Mary agreed with a wide smile. "Thank you, Suzie."

"You just stay out here and enjoy the view," Suzie encouraged her. "I'll bring everything to you."

"Okay, I will," Mary said as she gazed out over the glittering water. "I can't complain about the view, that's for sure."

Suzie ducked back into the house. As soon as she was inside she ran to her room and grabbed her cell phone. She dialed Paul's number. She could only hope that he would be awake early even though it was his first day off the boat.

"Hello?" he finally answered groggily.

"Paul, I need you," she said urgently.

"Oh baby, I need you, too," he mumbled half-asleep.

"Paul! Be serious!" Suzie said sharply.

"What? What is it? Are you in trouble?" he asked, suddenly wide awake.

"No, I'm not in trouble, but my surprise party is," Suzie sighed. "I'm sorry for waking you, it's just that I don't know who else to ask for help."

"You can always ask me for help, Suzie," Paul

said firmly. “What can I do?”

“Mary and Wes are on the outs, so now she wants to spend the day with me. But I'm supposed to be picking up Ben and Cathy from the airport in two hours,” she explained as she walked cautiously back towards the kitchen.

“Wow, that is a problem,” he said. “Would you like me to pick them up?”

“Would you?” she asked warmly. “That would help me out so much.”

“Of course, and if there's anything else that you need, just let me know,” he replied. “I think it's amazing that after all you went through yesterday you're still sticking with the party today.”

“Well, it's her first birthday away from Kent, and she needs to have it even more now that Wes is being such a jerk,” she sighed.

“Now, to be fair she did steal his gun,” Paul pointed out.

“Paul, I don't need you getting all

brotherhood of man on me right now," Suzie said. "I just need to get things together for Mary."

"Don't worry," Paul laughed. "Wes is being flat out stupid if he's passing up on a chance to spend time with Mary. I'll get the kids from the airport, just text them and let them know that it will be me picking them up."

"Okay, I will," Suzie sighed. "Thanks Paul, and sorry for being so out of sorts this morning."

"Don't apologize to me, sweetheart, I love you no matter what kind of sorts you're in," he replied lovingly. Suzie smiled to herself. It was nice to be reminded how lucky she was. But it stung a little to think that Mary was not getting the same kind of treatment. She decided to call Wes and give him a piece of her mind. She dialed his number, but it went straight to voicemail. She was just pouring some pancake batter into the pan when Mary stuck her head inside the house.

"Suzie, I'm going to get dressed, let me know if you need help with breakfast."

“Okay, I've got it covered,” Suzie smiled at her. Soon she had a plate filled with fluffy pancakes. She was fairly proud of them as she wasn't always the best cook. Just then she remembered to send the text to Benjamin and Catherine. She knew that they were probably already on the plane. She hoped that they would get the text when they landed. She prepared two plates for breakfast, and then heard a knock at the door. She walked over to the door and opened it to find Jason and Kirk standing outside. Suzie felt her heart skip a beat. She wondered if there had been a problem with Mary being in possession of the gun.

“Morning, Suzie,” Jason said as he took his hat off. He ran his hand back through his short red hair. “We wanted to check in with you two and make sure you're doing okay. I know today is Mary's birthday.”

“How nice,” Mary said as she stepped up behind Suzie. “Come in, have some breakfast,” she offered warmly. Jason glanced over at Kirk who nodded eagerly.

"It smells delicious," Kirk said.

"There is plenty," Suzie said in a welcoming tone and opened the door further so that they could step inside. Soon, all four of them were on the porch sharing breakfast.

"How did things go at the station?" Suzie asked.

"Larry gave a full confession," Jason said. "He even detailed how he took the screws out of the balcony. He used a ladder and climbed up, took the screws out, and climbed back down. Then, in the middle of the night he threw pistachio shells up on the balcony to get Warren to come outside. He said he waved and hollered as if he was in trouble to get Warren to lean forward against the railing. After that he fled off down the beach."

"He would have gotten away with it," Kirk said. "There was no physical evidence. He didn't even leave a fingerprint on the balcony, he never touched it, just the screws which he took with him. If it wasn't for the three of you getting in the middle of things, Warren Blasser's death would have been ruled an accident."

"I'm just glad that his family will get some closure," Mary said sadly.

"Listen to us talking about murder on Mary's birthday," Jason said with a shake of his head. "Today should be a happy day."

"With good friends and good food how could it not be?" Mary asked. She seemed to be in a much better mood. Suzie was glad that they had stopped by.

Chapter Fifteen

After Suzie had cleaned up from breakfast, she hid in her room to make a few phone calls.

"I need the cake to be delivered," she explained to the baker. "If you can have it here by about five that would be perfect. Of course I'll pay extra." Once the cake delivery was settled she placed a call to the caterers to make sure that the food would be ready to go by five. When she stepped out of her room she found Mary standing outside of it.

"What are you up to?" she asked suspiciously. "You've been sneaking around all day."

"Nothing," Suzie said innocently. "I was just making arrangements to meet with Paul later this evening."

"Oh," Mary nodded a little. She did her best to hide her disappointment. Suzie was just about to come up with even more excuses when her phone began ringing.

"I have to take this, I'm sorry, Mary," Suzie said as she ducked back into her room. It was Paul.

"Hello?" she whispered into the phone.

"Suzie, why are you still at Dune House?" he asked. "I'm here with Benjamin and Catherine."

"What?" Suzie glanced at her watch. "Oh no, I'm sorry! I lost track of time!"

"Well, if you come out you're going to see us. Do you want me to take them to lunch and come back in a little bit?" he asked.

"No, actually, just bring them in the back," Suzie said. "Give me five minutes."

"Okay," Paul replied before he hung up the phone.

Suzie rushed back to Mary's side. "Ready to go to a movie?" she asked.

"Really?" Mary smiled with excitement.

"Yes, absolutely," Suzie said. "Let's go right now, not a moment to waste."

"Did you even check the times?" Mary asked with some confusion.

"Sure I did," Suzie assured her. "Wait for me on the porch," Suzie instructed. "I just have to grab my purse."

"Don't worry about it, I'll drive and I'll pay," Mary said. "Let's go or we'll miss the previews."

"No way, you can't pay on your birthday," Suzie said. "You get the car started, I'll be right out."

"Okay, okay, but hurry," Mary said as she stepped out onto the porch. As soon as she closed the door, Suzie rushed to the back door. She opened it to find Paul, Benjamin, and Catherine standing outside.

"Oh, it's so good to see you!" she said as she gave them both a quick hug. "I'm sorry to do this, but things haven't worked out the way I planned. I need to get you upstairs and hidden away before your mother sees you."

"It's okay, Aunt Suzie," Benjamin said and

hugged her. Catherine gave her another tight hug.

"Is there anything that we can do to help?" she asked hopefully.

"Actually," Suzie glanced between the two of them. "If you wouldn't mind, I could really use some help with decorating the dining room. I won't be able to if I'm spending time with Mary."

"No problem," Catherine said with a smile. "We'd be happy to help."

"I can take them anywhere they need to go," Paul added. "Just go enjoy your time with Mary."

"Thank you so much," Suzie sighed.

"Suzie?" Mary called out as she stuck her head in the front door. "Did you find your purse?"

Suzie gasped and herded Benjamin and Catherine into the pantry.

"Not yet!" Suzie called back shakily.

"Well, it's right here," Mary said as she picked up Suzie's purse which had been sitting on the kitchen island. Paul was crouched down behind it.

"Oh, silly me," Suzie said. "Let's go!"

"Suzie, are you sure that you're okay?" Mary asked. "Yesterday was quite traumatic, maybe we should just stay in."

"Nonsense," Suzie said. "Let's get going," she nearly pushed Mary out through the front door. The rest of the afternoon was a whirlwind of Suzie sneaking off to make phone calls. Mary was exasperated by the time the movie was over and they had finished lunch.

"Really Suzie, if you'd rather be with Paul it's fine," Mary said with a shake of her head.

"The only person I want to be with on your birthday is you," Suzie insisted. "But not with that hair," she added.

"What?" Mary asked with surprise. She had worn the same hairstyle for a very long time.

"That's my birthday gift to you Mary, a trip to the hair salon," Suzie said. "I'm going to let you get your hair done while I cook you a nice dinner at home. Louis said he will give you a ride home when you are done."

"Okay, I guess," Mary said with a slight frown. Then she shook her head and smiled. "Thank you, Suzie," she said warmly.

"You deserve it, Mary," Suzie said. Once she had made the arrangements with the hairstylist and pleaded with her to delay her until the time of the party, Suzie sent a text to Louis to let him know that Mary would be waiting for him. Then she rushed back to Dune House to help with the final party preparations and greet the guests. She had invited just about the entire town. As everyone began to arrive, she noticed that Wes was missing. Suzie tried to call Wes to see if he was going to be there. His phone went to voicemail. She growled with frustration.

"What's wrong?" Paul asked.

"I can't believe he's not here yet," Suzie said as she paced back and forth in the foyer.

"It's okay, Suzie," Paul said in an attempt to soothe her. "I'm sure he'll be here. Something must have come up."

"He better be dead," Suzie muttered. "Or I'll kill him myself."

Paul raised his hands and backed away a few steps. "Scary," he said.

"It's her birthday," Suzie grumbled. "Her first one since she got away from that beast. She will be hurt if he doesn't show and I will be so furious with him."

"Wow," Paul chuckled. "I've never seen this side of you, Suzie," he stepped closer to her. "I think I like it."

"Not now, Paul," she huffed and then peered out the front window. "Unbelievable," she muttered just as a text came through from Louis to say that he and Mary were on their way. "Mary's on her way, Wes is going to ruin the surprise," Suzie said with frustration.

"Suzie remember, this is for Mary," Paul said gently. "Let's just try to have fun, and maybe not so much talk about murder with the cop here," he tilted his head towards Jason who had walked out to the foyer.

"Murder?" he asked and looked between the two. "I thought this was a party?"

"You're right, you're right," Suzie sighed. "Okay, everybody hide!" she said as she headed into the kitchen. Benjamin and Catherine were ducked behind the front desk. Mary opened the door. Suzie was surprised by the bobbed hairstyle she had chosen. It suited her, and made her eyes shine.

"Surprise!" Suzie shouted, signaling everyone to jump up from behind the furniture. Mary gasped and jumped backwards a few feet.

"What have you done, Suzie?" she roared. "Benjamin, Catherine?" she cried out. "Oh my babies!" she said happily and rushed over to them. She smothered them in hugs and kisses. Suzie couldn't stop smiling. Until she heard Wes shuffle in behind her.

"It's about time," she said to him sharply and

fixed him with a glare.

Wes shot back a harsh look. “I'm sorry, I got held up.”

“Wes! Do you see what Suzie has done?” Mary said, laughing with joy.

“I'm sorry I was late,” he said. “Here, I brought you a present,” Wes was still eying Suzie with some annoyance.

“Thank you,” Mary said sweetly. Suzie noticed Benjamin watching Wes closely, before he whispered to his sister.

“Open it,” Wes insisted. “I can't wait for you to see it.”

Mary smiled and began carefully unwrapping the gift. Inside the paper was a wooden box, with intricate designs on the sides.

“It's beautiful,” Mary said.

“No, no, you have to open the box,” Wes grinned.

Mary raised her eyebrows and lifted the lid on

the box. Inside was what appeared to be a painting of the outside of Dune House, framed by the clear blue sea.

"It's a puzzle," Wes blurted out. "I know how much you like them, so I thought you might like this."

"I do," Mary said with a gasp. "It's perfect, Wes," she hugged him tightly.

"I'm glad you like it," Wes said proudly. "I really wanted it to be a surprise and it was quite an adventure to get it done. I had to hunt down some real artists, and you know how unreliable they can be."

"Is this what you've been keeping a secret?" Mary asked with surprise.

"Well, I thought it would be a simple present at first, but there was a lot more to it than I expected. I'm sorry that I've been so preoccupied, I just wanted it to be a surprise."

"It is," Mary said warmly. "A beautiful one. I don't think I've ever had a more wonderful birthday," she admitted. Suzie felt a sense of warmth wash over her. It had been touch and go for a while, but it seemed the party was going to be a success.

Once the party was in full swing Suzie felt a sense of relief. She could see that Mary was having a wonderful time with Wes, Catherine, and Benjamin. The rest of the guests seemed to be enjoying the food and beverages as well as the company. Suzie stepped out onto the porch to grab a breath of fresh air. She heard footsteps just behind her.

"A chance to be alone," Paul said as he slid his arms around her. "You did a great job, Suzie."

"I never could have done it without you," Suzie said with a grim smile. "This party was almost a disaster."

"It could never be a disaster with you in charge," Paul said firmly. "You gave her a great birthday, Suzie."

"She deserves it," Suzie said with a fond smile.

“So, now that Wes and Mary are lost in romance again, maybe we could try for some of our own?” he suggested.

“That sounds like a lovely idea to me, Paul,” Suzie replied. She smiled as he pulled her close.

The End

More Cozy Mysteries by Cindy Bell

Dune House Cozy Mysteries

Seaside Secrets

Boats and Bad Guys

Treasured History

Hidden Hideaways

Dodgy Dealings

Sage Gardens Cozy Mysteries

Birthdays Can Be Deadly

Money Can Be Deadly

Wendy the Wedding Planner Cozy Mysteries

Matrimony, Money and Murder

Chefs, Ceremonies and Crimes

Knives and Nuptials

Mice, Marriage and Murder

Heavenly Highland Inn Cozy Mysteries

Murdering the Roses

Dead in the Daisies

Killing the Carnations

Drowning the Daffodils

Suffocating the Sunflowers

Books, Bullets and Blooms

A Deadly serious Gardening Contest

A Bridal Bouquet and a Body

Bekki the Beautician Cozy Mysteries

Hairspray and Homicide

A Dyed Blonde and a Dead Body

Mascara and Murder

Pageant and Poison

Conditioner and a Corpse

Mistletoe, Makeup and Murder

Hairpin, Hair Dryer and Homicide

Blush, a Bride and a Body

Shampoo and a Stiff

Cosmetics, a Cruise and a Killer

Lipstick, a Long Iron and Lifeless

Camping, Concealer and Criminals